Mrs. Macabre And The Fear King

The Mrs. Macabre Chronicles, Volume 3

Austin Ray Bouse

Published by Austin Bouse, 2023.

MRS. MACABRE AND THE FEAR KING

First edition. October 2, 2023.

ISBN: 979-8223506942

Written by Austin Ray Bouse.

Also by Austin Ray Bouse

The Mrs. Macabre Chronicles
Mrs. Macabre
Merry Christmas, Mrs. Macabre
Mrs. Macabre And The Fear King

Table of Contents

To my parents and my Universal family. Speacial
thanks to Francesca Leon, my editor, who consistantly
makes my words better.

1.
THE TELL-TALE
HEART

It came without warning. If you have ever had a panic attack, then I am sorry to say that you know precisely how Jane Gracey felt. In fact, you may wish to not be reminded of how it felt, in which case, we shall meet again in a few pages time.

If you have *not* experienced a panic attack, this is how it felt for her.

The day had begun just as nearly every day of her life had. Her and her identical twin sister, Catie, had woken up annoyed that it was a school day instead of the weekend. The only comfort that they received was that they would see their friend Bram during class and that their Friday and Saturday nights would be filled with trips to the Hallowland with the witch Mrs. Macabre and her spooky found family. They were only allowed to see her on non-school nights. Though Mrs. Macabre was known for her love of fun and mischief, she was also known for her love of education. "After all," she would tell them, "how else would Vlad the Impaler have known how long his stakes should have been if not for education?"

And so, they boarded the bus that would take them to school and proceeded to be educated. It was only until they got to Mr. O'Brien's English class-which just happened to be her favorite- that Jane began to sense something was wrong. What was wrong, she could not put words to, all she felt was a kind of itch inside her mind that she could not scratch. Her hands curled into fists on her desk as the itch grew and grew.

The florescent lights above her seemed to brighten, making the white walls of the classroom glow to the point where her eyes began to squint.

Mr. O'Brien's lecture on Rudyard Kipling's *The Jungle Book* was being drowned out by the sound of chalk hitting against the blackboard. With every letter he made, it cut through the board like a knife, sending sharp screams into her ears.

Small clouds of white dust bloomed from the chalk like snow.

She looked around to Catie, Bram, and even her bully, Courtney Clearwater to see if they could hear the awful shrieks as well or if they too were blinded by the whiteness of the room, but they were not. They, along with the rest of the class sat still in their desks, some paying attention, others trying their hardest not to fall asleep, all of them acted as if nothing in the world was wrong.

You can do this, Jane told herself. *Just ignore it. Don't let it happen again. Ignore it.* But try as she might, she could not ignore it for much longer. The sound of the chalk against the blackboard was accompanied by another sound. It was like the ticking of a clock, a sound that she was not unfamiliar with.

The clock above Mr. O'Brien's head was an instrument that could be heard quite loudly in the silence of tests and other assignments. But this ticking was different. It did not have the clarity of the clock in the room, but more of a far away sound. The sound not of a clock exactly, but of a watch wrapped in cotton. A chill went up her spine as she realized what the source of the ticking was. It was her own heartbeat.

She swallowed, but her throat felt as dry as it had ever been. Her palms were damp as she gripped her fists tighter, digging her nails into the skin. Her right leg pumped up and down with the speed of a locomotive engine. The ticking of her heart grew louder and louder in her ears. Her front teeth pierced her bottom lip almost to the point of bleeding. Her heartbeat grew faster and faster, louder and louder, until. . . .

She shot up from her desk. As she stormed her way through the isles she could barely hear Mr. O'Brien's muffled query of, "Is everything okay, Jane?" But she could not answer him. Not because she didn't have an answer, but because instead of giving him an explanation, she would scream. She saw flashes of Catie and Bram's furrowed brows and Courtney's horrible smirking pink lips of spite. She did not care. All she cared about was getting out of there as fast as she could.

Once she exited the classroom, she ran as fast as she could to the restroom. It seemed so far away, the hallway grew longer with every second. Her shoes echoed against the walls as if she were in a tunnel. Finally, she made it. She threw the door open and sprinted into one of the stalls, locking it. She bent down over the toilet, hoping something would purge itself out of her, but nothing came. She tried again, but still nothing emptied out of her throat. *Please*! Her voice screamed inside of her. *Please get this feeling out of me!*

Get out!

Get out!

GET OUT!

The hideous beating of her heart continued to plague her ears. She slammed her back against one of the walls and slowly slid down onto the floor, crying. Trapped in the stall like a prison of her own making.

"Jane?" She heard Catie's voice call to her with the squeak of the restroom door. "What's wrong? Is it happening again?"

"Is she okay?" Bram's voice called from outside.

"I-I- don't know," Jane sobbed, the words pulled their way out of her mouth like a marathon runner going up a steep hill.

"Can you let me in?" Her sister knocked on the door, which was as loud as the beating inside her head. "Please?"

Jane could not move. She wanted to stay in this box for all eternity. She refused to be like Pandora and open it, flooding the world with chaos. "I-I don't know," she stammered again. Her breath going in and out with the force of a hurricane.

"Please, Jane?" Catie pleaded with her. "It's me."

Jane sat still for a few moments longer until, finally, she mustered the strength to open the lock quickly like the thing had sharp teeth and could bite her at any moment. Catie opened the door and ran in, not even assessing the environment. She dove down to her sister and hugged her. "It's okay," she whispered in her ear. "Everything is okay."

Jane sobbed and sobbed, trembling in her sister's shoulders. The beating still continued. She thought she was going to die.

She didn't know how, she didn't know why, all she knew was that she was coming to an end, unraveling into Catie's arms.

"It's okay," Catie whispered.

The beat grew softer.

"It's okay."

And softer.

"It's okay."

Her breathing slowed.

"It's okay."

The storm was passing.

"It's okay."

She was in the stall of a bathroom.

"It's okay."

She felt the tile underneath her.

"It's okay."

She was in her school.

"It's okay."

She was with her identical twin sister.

"It's okay."

She was going to live.

"It's okay."

The ticking stopped.

For now.

Jane's panic attack loomed over the day with the darkness of a shadow. Once she had returned to Mr. O'Brien's class, she was forced to make some kind of excuse for not feeling well after the teacher had asked her with great concern, "Is everything all right?" She was forced to stare into the eyes of her fellow classmates as they either tried to avoid her gaze or thought she had completely lost her mind. Courtney's smile was the worst of them all. Hers was a smile of such righteous satisfaction it nearly made Jane want to strangle her. But that would have made matters even worse. The damage was done. This had been the second panic attack she had been plagued with in a month. It was far worse than the last, at least the first time it only amounted to tears. This time she had made a scene.

No, not a scene, that was too polite of a word for it. The word that Courtney would use behind her back would be *show* or *drama*, something to gain attention. Yes, that was it. That was why she had behaved in such an extreme way, like someone from a bad movie, it was to get attention. It wasn't the fact that she had seen things and had nearly been killed within the past few months to make her behave this way. No one in her class could know what it was like to feel the cold grip of the Weeping Widow's long, skeleton hands. No one in her class could know what it was like to race through watery depths to save your sister from drowning. No one could know the fear that grips a heart when they discover that their loved one will be burned alive. Catie and Bram might, they were there of course, but they were both braver than her. They always had been.

The Gracey family sat together at the dinner table, eating spaghetti and salad. Mr. and Mrs. Gracey each took turns on what their day had been like- just another day at the office for their father and another day grooming dogs for their mother. When asked how the twins' day went, Catie quickly responded with "Fine. Everything went fine."

"Oh?" Mrs. Gracey asked, interested. "That's unusual for you. The best we can get out of you two is a mumble."

"Fine," Mr. Gracey responded with a smile. "Must have been an amazing day, then!" He glanced at his wife and they both chuckled. They continued on talking about work or how the lawn should be taken care of, as they always did. No need to further inquire into their daughters' lives. Fine was fine by them.

Jane looked over at Catie and her sister gave her a small smile. Jane was grateful for how quick Catie had been to cover for her. She knew what would happen if her parents found out about that day. The conversation would have gone something like this:

"How was your day, girls?" Mrs. Gracey would ask.

"Terrible," Jane would say quietly. Her head down, continuing to eat her dinner.

"Oh?" Her mother would ask, concerned, "How so?"

"I had another panic attack. Worse this time."

"Another?" Mr. Gracey would say, alarmed. "What do you mean by another?"

"I mean I had a panic attack about a few weeks ago, but this one was so much worse. I felt like I was going to die."

"Did you know about this?" Mrs. Gracey would ask her sister, anger rising in her voice.

"We didn't want to upset you," Catie would say sheepishly.

Both of their parents would let out long, tired sighs.

"How could you keep this from us?" Mr. Gracey would say.

"You got this from me, didn't you?" Mrs. Gracey's eyes would brim with tears. "I was afraid this was going to happen. I've always been so anxious."

"This is selfish of you to keep this from us."

"Should have seen a doctor."

"We're your parents!"

"You need to see a therapist. I'm calling a therapist."

"How could you let yourself get so upset over nothing?"

"Maybe they can get you on some type of medication."

"You've always been so much of a handful. Both of you."

"It's all my fault."

"Why couldn't you be normal for once?"

"It's all my fault."

"Nuisance. The both of you."

"Should never have let you watch all those scary movies."

"Should never have had kids in the first place."

That is what they would have said. Or, at least that is what Jane *thought* they would have said. In truth, she had no way of knowing how her parents would have reacted to the day's incident, but the truth didn't matter. What mattered was the fear. The fear that all those things that ran in her head could be true. And what *could* be true is always more terrifying than the truth itself. Jane wrapped the spaghetti around her fork like the scream that was caught in her throat and ate it.

That night, Jane could barely sleep. She tossed and turned, her mind unable to rest itself. The memories of the day swirled behind her eyelids like a cyclone. How the walls of the classroom seemed to blind her, how the sound of the chalk hitting the board pierced her ears, how her heart felt as if it were going to burst out of her chest. Shame came over her in waves, in and out, she wondered how long it would take until the entire school knew about her panic attacks, how Courtney would spread the gossip around the halls like wildfire. Or worse yet, if it were to happen again, how long would it take until one of her teachers told her parents? Then she would feel even worse. Not only was she having these horrible feelings, but she'd been keeping them from her own mother and father.

"What's wrong?" Catie's half-asleep voice broke through the storm.

"Nothing," Jane said, quickly. "Just having a little insomnia, that's all. Go back to sleep."

"I know your insomnia roll. That's not it. You have something on your mind. Is it about today?"

"What do you mean? What happened today?"

She heard her sister lift herself up from her bed. "Don't play dumb. About your panic attack. It's bothering you."

The jig was up. Of course her mom and dad weren't able to catch it, but her twin, her mirror could see through her as if she were a clear pane of glass. Jane sighed and lifted herself up as well."Yeah. I'm scared."

"I know," Catie said softly. "Do you want to talk about it?"

"What's there to talk about," she gave a wry chuckle. "It's a problem. If it gets worse, I'll deal with it."

"I don't think this is something that you can *deal* with."

"Compared to all the other stuff we've had to deal with? The Weeping Widow? Vampires? *The Grim Reaper*? I think I've got this."

"I meant see someone. Like a therapist or taking medication," Catie said with a sigh, again she was able to see through the act. "It's not something to be ashamed of. People do it all the time."

"I'm not a ashamed of it," Jane snapped, to her surprise. "I just don't think I *need* those things, you know?"

"I think you do. This could get worse."

"Not if I work at it."

"How are you going to work at it?" Catie's voice grew tighter, it was the biggest sign that she was growing even more frustrated.

"Don't worry about it. I can ignore it," Jane felt her hands starting to sweat.

"But I *am* worried Jane. You can't ignore this away!"

"Just. . . just shut up, okay? Go back to sleep! I don't want to talk about this anymore!" Jane landed on her bed and turned her back towards her sister. She heard Catie give an exasperated sigh and then she too fell back onto her bed. Jane shut her eyes tight again, now her worries were tainted with anger. Therapy would cost too much money. It would bother her parents too much, they'd ask her over and over how she was feeling like they were stepping through a mine field. Besides, she could handle it herself, right? She could control her emotions just as easy as walking, right? It wouldn't be that much of a problem? It wouldn't be that hard?

. . . Right?

She rolled over on her back. Who was she kidding? This wasn't going to work. The panic attacks were too powerful. She'd never be able to control them. She'd live the ret of her life freaking out over the simplest things like a bird chirping or water running. The smallest, dumbest things would set her off. Everyone around her would laugh and she'd grow up to be that one crazy lady who has a meltdown at the drop of a hat. It was useless. She didn't need therapy or medication. The only thing that could cure her would be. . .

Magic.

She bolted upright in bed. "Catie?" She asked. "Are you awake?"

"I'm not if you want to argue some more," Catie grumbled.

"What if Mrs. Macabre could fix me?"

"How do you mean?" Catie rolled over, facing her.

"What if she could fix me with like, a spell or a potion or something?" She smiled.

"She's a witch not a doctor."

"But isn't that kind of the same thing?" Jane looked at the clock on the nightstand between their beds. It was ten minutes past midnight, the gate to the Hallowland would be open for another fifty minutes. "Why don't we just ask her if she could?"

"I don't know about this," Catie scratched her head, "we don't know what kind of side effects her magic could have."

"We don't know if we don't ask! We were going to see her and the others, anyway!"

Catie sat in bed for a moment, staring at the window across the room in thought. Jane could sense the wheels inside her head, that machine of hers whirling around like clockwork. ". . . Okay," she finally said and got out of bed.

"Yes!" Jane danced around in her bed. "You won't regret this!"

Catie groaned as she went to the closet to change her clothes. Jane immediately opened the nightstand drawer and pulled out a coffin-shaped box. It was where they kept all the mementos from over the years, including a piece of straw from Mrs. Macabre's magical broomstick. Their key to the Hallowland itself. Jane's heart beat faster with every second, but to her relief, it was not from anxiety. This time, it was from excitement.

2.
THE MORBID MARKET

Before they crossed over the gate into the Hallowland, the Gracey twins felt that it was only right to invite Bram. They had first thought it would be best to throw small rocks at his bedroom window to get his attention, but decided on a more utilitarian approach by calling his phone. Upon waking up and opening his window, the twins described to him their current predicament and, to no surprise, Bram was more than willing to visit the Hallowland once again. He quickly put on more appropriate attire than his pajamas, fetched his testosterone kit, and made his way down to the lawn of his house from the window. He had grown quite good at it since their first adventure together.

Once they had entered the strange black curtain of the gate, saw the flashes of magical green lightning, and felt the coolness of the wind against their faces, the trio found themselves on the side of a mountain. Jane looked over and stared in wonder at the various peaks that jutted out of a carpet of swirling fog in front of them. The stars twinkled in the night sky and the moon shone high above like a spotlight. Then she noticed something strange in the air. At first she thought it was the howling of a werewolf nearby or the moaning of the wind, but it was too melodic for it to be either of those things. The sound was not moving towards or away from them, yet it sounded muffled, contained somehow. She turned and she, along with her friends, saw that Mrs. Macabre's manor had parked itself just several feet away.

They went up the front steps of the coffin-shaped house and knocked on the door. Mrs. Mirth, who was Mrs. Macabre's wife, answered it. Her mouth moved, but it was unclear what she was saying, however it *was* clear what the strange sound was. Somewhere deep within the manor, someone was playing a pipe organ. It's metallic melody blared throughout the seemingly endless funnel that made up the foyer of the house, playing the same notes over and over again.

"*We can't hear you!*" Jane cried out to their host as the children held their hands over their ears, their faces wincing as if they had tasted something sour. Mrs. Mirth, who they had just noticed was wearing fuzzy earmuffs over her long blue hair, thought for a moment of what to do. She then smiled as she realized something, held up her finger, and shut the door.

"And I thought *I* was bad at music class," Bram said rubbing his ears.

"Mom and Dad should hear that if they think we play *The Misfits* too loud," Catie said to Jane.

The door opened once again and Mrs. Mirth quickly gave each of them a pair of earmuffs. They placed them on their heads and were relieved that the music had died down. "I hope that makes things better," Mr. Mirth's voice spoke to them as if she were whispering right into their ears instead of being feet in front of them.

"I, uh, I think so," Jane said, not wanting to let on how unnerved she was by the magic earmuffs. "Mrs. Mirth, we need to speak to Mrs. Macabre. Is she busy?"

"She's the one playing the music," she smiled cocking a thumb indoors. "She loves this one. It's our song, you know," she leaned against her cane and sighed with love.

"That's. . . . cute," Jane continued. "But we really need to speak to her. Or, more like I need to speak with her. They've come along to support," she gestured to her sister and Bram.

"Why, of course. Do come in, dears! Do come in!" Mrs. Mirth rushed them in, hugging them all, then shutting the door behind her. "She's in the Music Room obviously," she said with a small giggle.

The children looked around and saw the skeletons and furniture moving ever so slightly as the organ continued to play. Above them, they heard the purring of doors as the floors went up and up, rattling like loose teeth. Somewhere off to the side, their friend Jack Lantern came running across the foyer.

"Hi, Jack!" They all said and waved at him.

"MAKE IT STOP! MAKE IT STOP! MAKE IT STOP!" He shrieked as he held his gloved hands against his pumpkin head, the candle inside it glowed with nervous energy. Even with the earmuffs on, it was apparently too much for the scarecrow.

"Some people just don't see the romance in it, I guess," Mrs. Mirth shrugged. "Come on, then. I'll guide you up there," she gestured for them to follow her as she limped her way to the elevator nearby. Once they had gotten inside, she closed the iron gate of the lift and pressed the button that lead to their destination. As they made their way up, the music grew louder with every level, the elevator rattled along with it, shuddering in a way that made it seem just as anxious as Jack below. Mrs. Mirth continued to hum the song as it repeated itself, moving her head side to side, like it was a waltz. The children looked at each other in disbelief. They had seen some strange things during their Hallowland adventures, but this was certainly the most surreal.

The elevator reached the requested floor and Mrs. Mirth opened the gate. They made their way down the winding corridor which the Gracey twins couldn't help but feel nostalgic for their first time in the magical house. They turned a corner and saw their other monster friend, Arachne scuttling across the ceiling with all of her legs.

"*It's driving me up the walls!*" The spider-woman shouted, holding her earmuffs tightly with her hands, her eight eyes shut even more tightly together.

"Ah, here we are," Mrs. Mirth said as they reached the door marked MUSIC ROOM. She opened it and Jane saw that the pipe organ was at the end of a room filled with all manner of musical instruments. Violins, cellos, oboes, harps, harpsichords, flutes, and accordions lined the room. There were so many that Jane couldn't possibly believe that Mrs. Macabre played all of them. In fact, knowing her the way she did, she probably never took one lesson. In all likelihood, the witch kept them purely for decorative purposes. As the children moved closer, they saw that the enormous organ was adorned with long strands of cobwebs and lit candles. Spiders came crawling out of the metal pipes, nearly dancing their way down, just as Mrs. Macabre's black-nailed pale fingers danced along the keys and knobs of the instrument.

"Darling!" Mrs. Mirth yelled through the music, though Mrs. Macabre herself continued to play with her earmuffs on. "*Darling!*" She shouted again, tapping her on the shoulder. The music immediately stopped as Mrs. Macabre looked at her partner, startled. She was wearing her standard Victorian black gown with her equally dark hair tied at the back of her head. Her eyes quickly looked from Mrs. Mirth to the children.

"My marvelous misfits!" She gasped and smiled, her black lipstick widening. She learned over from her bench and gave each of them a hug. "What brings you here?"

"Well, Mrs. Macabre," Jane said, slightly embarrassed. "I was wondering if you could help me with something?"

"I'm all ears," she said, taking off her muffs. Jane relayed to her the story of her recent panic attacks and how they were getting worse "Oh, dear," the witch frowned, looking at Mrs. Mirth, who shared the same expression. "That does sound terrible. But how can I be of service to you?"

"I was hoping you had a spell or some kind of potion to make them go away?" Jane asked with her heart swelling in hopeful anticipation.

"Oh, my love," Mrs. Macabre held her hands. "I understand why you would think such a thing. In fact, I appreciate that you came to me of all people during your time of need. But I am afraid that my magic is unable to accomplish such a task."

"What do you mean?" Jane asked, looking confused.

"Can't you whip up something?" Catie chimed in. "Like the time you gave us that potion that turned us into vampires?"

"You can transform into a raven," Bram added. "Why can't you take away her anxiety?"

"Magic is not that simple, my dears," Mrs. Macabre sighed. "It can be used to change many things. It can change your appearance such as when we were at the Vampire Ball, Catherine, or how I can transform into a raven, Abraham. It can even be used to heal wounds as it did with those home remedies when you were attacked by those gremlins, Jane. But it cannot change who you *are*. For instance, magic cannot turn Lara disabled to able-bodied," she gestured to Mrs. Mirth.

"Nor would I want it to," her partner smiled.

"I have even tried to use magic in that way during my darkest hour," Mrs. Macabre said gravely. "But that created the Weeping Widow and we all know how that turned out." A cold shudder went through most of them as the memories of the Widow- the ghost forged from Mrs. Macabre's darkest parts of herself- came back to them like a bad dream.

Jane stood silent for a moment, not knowing what to do. Her hopes had been deflated and now what were her only options? How could she conquer what she was afraid of? *Why* was she afraid of these things when her entire identity was wrapped up in loving the things that go bump in the night? She had prayed for a quick and easy fix to her problems, but now, she was back to square one. Her eyes glanced to the sheet music in front of Mrs. Macabre. Above the repeating notes was the title *The Fear King Waltz*.

"Who is the Fear King?" she asked.

"Oh, him?" The witch glanced at the music, "he's just as the title suggests, the king of fears, or that's what *he* calls himself, at least. This piece was commissioned by him for the great composer Salazar Slime. A bit vain, if you ask me."

"But so romantic," Mrs. Mirth cooed and her partner kissed her hand.

"Do you think he could help me?" Jane's hope flicked once again inside of her.

"I don't think that would be a good idea, Jane," Mrs. Macabre said. "He's very mysterious, no one has ever seen him, in fact. Not to mention the treacherous Nightmare Jungle."

"What's that?" Catie asked, her intrigue over this new place and the possibility of Jane getting better growing with every moment.

"It is said that it was created by the Fear King himself," Mrs. Mirth answered. "It's filled with the most wild things the Hallowland has to offer and is shaped like a huge spiral around his castle. That is why the waltz repeats itself over and over again. It is an homage to one of the greatest natural wonders in existence."

"Mrs. Macabre, this is my chance!" Jane beamed up at her. "If anyone can fix my anxiety, it must be the Fear King!"

"Darling," Mrs. Macabre placed a hand on her shoulder. "I know you are excited by the prospect, but you don't know what's in that jungle. *I* don't know what's in there. It could be more dangerous than anything we've ever faced."

"More dangerous than you almost being burned alive by Father Christmas?" Bram asked.

"Or when Jane had to rescue you and I from the Grim Reaper all by herself?" Catie stepped forward.

"Or the *Weeping Widow*?" Jane pressed, hoping their arguments would change her mind.

Mrs. Macabre gave a small sigh and looked at Mrs. Mirth, not knowing what to do. The two witches continued to gaze at one another, almost as if they were reading each other's thoughts. It reminded Jane of how she and Catie often exchanged words without even uttering a sentence, or how their mother could communicate so much to their father with a single look. She supposed that it was an ability that one acquires when one has loved another for so long. Love could be its own magic, it seemed. A magic that came with its own spells.

"Oh, all right," she finally relented, rubbing her eyes together. The children all cheered. "But you *must* not leave my sight and you *must* do as I say," she added sternly. "You know how relaxed I am with all of you, since I believe all children should have autonomy over their lives. But this might be the rare case where I have to watch you with the eyes of a vulture."

"Oh, thank you, Mrs. Macabre!" Jane said, embracing her. "Thank you so much!"

"Of course, my dear," Mrs. Macabre held her tight. "Of course," she smiled knowing that she had made a child happy. A task that she felt was the greatest magic of all.

They reached their destination the next morning. As Mrs. Macabre's manor traversed the terrain of the Hallowland on its giant bird legs, the children barely noticed as they slept in rooms that looked identical to their own bedrooms. Upon waking, they went down to the kitchen and the entire found family of children, witches, and monsters had a fine breakfast of toast with Jersey Devil jam and a side of beastly bacon as they listened to the soothing sounds of the rain beginning to tap on the windows. It reminded Jane of Elvira, Mrs. Macabre's talking black cat, who would often spend her breakfast making sarcastic comments in between bits of raw fish in her bowl in the corner. She missed her very much.

Once they were all full, they met in the foyer. "Now, children," Mrs. Macabre announced to them, "if we're going to trek the often difficult journey through the Nightmare Jungle, then we are going to need the appropriate attire!" She reached for her black broom that she kept in the umbrella stand by the front door. She plucked a piece of straw from the bottom of it and placed it inside a pocket of her dress. She closed her eyes for a brief moment, snapped her fingers, and then, right in front of them, her clothes transformed, like a gothic Cinderella. Her black dress and shoes became a safari outfit. Her small hat and veil turned into a pith helmet. She tapped the broom against the floor and it became a walking stick, the only sign of its original form was the raven skull that was its handle.

"Cool!" Bram smiled, the Gracey twins briefly looked at each other, forgetting that he had never seen this particular act of magic before. "How do you do that?"

"It's easy," Catie said as she was given a piece of straw from Mrs. Macabre. "You just put it in your pocket, close your eyes, think of what you want to wear, and snap your fingers!"

Bram took the straw gently from the witch as if it were made of the most brittle glass. He tenderly placed it in his pocket, closed his eyes, and snapped his fingers, letting his imagination run wild. He opened them and looked to see that he was wearing a uniform of tweed with a bowtie and a vest.

A very professorial look that he very much appreciated, considering that he was the monster expert of the group.

Catie placed hers in her pocket, snapped, and soon transformed from her regular clothes to a black safari uniform similar to Mrs. Macabre, but hers was a pair of shorts and a button down shirt with pockets in them. Jane closed her eyes, snapped her fingers, and her uniform was nearly the same as her sister's.

"Splendid!" Mrs. Macabre smiled. "Who else would like to join us?" She turned to her compatriots.

"Well, I. . . I, uh," Jack said sheepishly. "I don't think I would do well in a place called the Nightmare Jungle, don't you think?" He chuckled, but his fear was evident.

"Don't worry, my dear," Mrs. Macabre patted him on the shoulder. "You can take care of the manor while we're gone." Jack's candle burned warmly inside his head.

"I think I'll stay here, if you don't mind," Mrs. Mirth said. "I don't think the jungle is very disabled friendly," she gestured to her crooked leg and her cane. "Besides, I can keep Jack company, since he gets scared being alone." She smiled towards the scarecrow and he gave her a small hug in return.

"Of course, my love," Mrs. Macabre kissed her partner on the lips.

"Guess, I'll go!" Arachne moved forward. "Gives me a chance to see the world and stretch my legs a bit after being cooped up in here for so long." She wobbled her eight legs in a kind of jittery dance.

"Very well!" Mrs. Macabre declared with her typical theatrical flourish. "Let's see what's out there!" She pulled the door open and what the children saw baffled them. The rain was pouring down even harder now than it was when they were at the breakfast table, but our three young heroes thought they saw a vast collection of rolling dark hills. Far cry from a jungle. But then, after they allowed their eyes to adjust, they realized that they were not looking at hills at all, but street vendors. Booths and dioramas made of wood, metal, and other materials filled their vision as far as they could see. It was so crowded and large that you would easily believe that you were looking at a small city of markets.

"What kind of a jungle is *this*?" Jane asked, perplexed.

"Oh, no, my dear," Mrs. Macabre chuckled. "This isn't the Nightmare Jungle, it's the Morbid Market!"

"The what?" They all asked in unison, partially from their own confusion and partially due to how hard the rain was coming down, it was very hard to hear what Mrs. Macabre was saying without her raising her voice.

"The Morbid Market!" She repeated cheerfully. "You see, once the Nightmare Jungle was created by the Fear King, it grew in reputation equally for its beauty and for its sense of danger. Explorers and daredevils alike wanted to test their skills against the jungle and make their way to the prize of the Fear King's castle. Naturally, every monster in the Hallowland who was selling anything from gargoyle hide to their mother's cookie recipe set up shop here. The Nightmare Jungle is just beyond here, "she stepped onto the front porch and beckoned the children and Arachne to follow her. "So long, my loves!" She waved to Mrs. Mirth and Jack and shut the door. She then raised her walking stick and it soon became an umbrella.

"Come along then," she told them. "Unless you'd rather start our adventure soaking wet."

"But, Mrs. Macabre," Catie said. "That's just a regular sized umbrella! How can we all fit underneath it?"

"My darling, Catherine," the witch said with a knowing smile. "After all our time together I am still surprised by how you underestimate my magic."

Catie, Bram, and Arachne all looked at each other and then, gingerly, took several steps closer to Mrs. Macabre. As they inched closer, they saw that the umbrella managed to cover them all without changing shape or size. The canopy rested above them perfectly, giving them enough room to walk and move as they weren't crammed in together like a coffin.

"Very, good, then. Now, if we all move together, I'm sure we won't have any trouble at all!" Mrs. Macabre said over the rain and they all moved as one down the steps of the manor and onto the wet grass.

They gazed back and forth as the Morbid Market surrounded them. Rugs made of skin for sale, teeth of all shapes and sizes, a headless vendor selling various noggins as if they were wigs, the salty scent of two-headed fish sizzling on a grill, a woman made completely of mushrooms selling her spores as ointments, two squat creatures- one atop the other- calling out to the highest bidder their services as husbands for the price of one, garments made of the finest spun snake, a demon selling a Hair-Be-Gone Flamethrower 666.

"Nineteen pentacles for this Fur-bearing Trout!"

"Bigfoot toenails! Get your Bigfoot toenails!"

"Mummy dust! Look good when you're alive *and* dead with authentic mummy dust!"

All this and more made the Morbid Market its own type of jungle. A jungle made of profit and materialism. "How are we going to find our way to the Nightmare Jungle in *this* madness?" Bram asked, a little excited and nervous by what was around him.

"Simple," Mrs. Macabre replied. "We'll just ask!" She walked over to a man with the head of an octopus. "Excuse me, sir, I was wondering if you could help us?" But all she got in response were a few angry pops of his tentacles, which she took as an answer in the resounding negative. "I have a question for you."

"Not unless you're going to buy something, honey," a panther woman said with a skeptical growl.

"Well, I won't be buying anything from *you*, thank you very much!" The witch said, curtly. She tried a faun. "Do you have a map that I could borrow?" But was nearly thrown off balance when a goblin pushed her out of the way to purchase one of the faun's homemade pelts. "Oh, for the love of Hades! DOES ANYONE KNOW WHICH WAY THE FEAR KING'S CASTLE IS?" She yelled as loud as she could and the entire market stopped. They all stared at them in a silence that soon grew to something eerie. It was if she had spoken some secret words that should never be uttered aloud, or at the very least, in this company. Only the rain continued to talk.

"Who?" A man with the head of an owl asked. It had been so quiet that the question nearly made our companions jump.

Mrs. Macabre cleared her throat. "I am Mrs. Lenore Macabre, Witch For Hire. My friends and I demand to see him. Once we know where the Nightmare Jungle is, of course."

"Why?" A little skeleton boy holding a large round lollipop asked. "Why do you want to see the Boogeyman?" His voice was soft and afraid.

"That business is our own. All that matters is how we get there. Now, if one of you would kindly point us in the right direction-"

"Doomed," a raspy voice cut her off. They all turned and, making her way towards them, was an elderly creature. The lumbering pile of rags made its way towards them, slowly but surely. She was a stocky woman with skin the color of a toad and the face of a turtle that peeked out of her wool hood. Her bottom lip nearly covered half of her face and her eyes were so squinted and small that they were barely visible within the wrinkles. Her long white hair hung in strands around her face in wet curls. Beads and trinkets decorated her muddy robes like a religious figure. Whoever she was, a sense of great importance followed her.

"What-" Mrs. Macabre started, clearing her throat again. "What was that?"

"Doomed," the Creature said again. "Those who seek the Fear King, they are doomed."

"Do you know him?" Jane asked, unnerved, but curious.

"Yes. But never seen him."

"Then how do you know him?" Arachne said.

"We all know Fear," the woman said, which sent a quiet chill through the entire market.

"Can you take us to the Nightmare Jungle?"

"Nay. Fairy Godmother don't go there. Fairy Godmother stay safe. Fairy Godmother is smart. Fairy Godmother is wise," the old woman spoke in a matter of fact tone.

"But we *have* to see him!" Jane pleaded. "He's the only one that can take away *my* fear!"

The Fairy Godmother made a noise that was either a cough or a chuckle. "Very well. Forward," she raised a lumpy finger behind her. "Right. Left. Right. There."

"Thank you," Mrs. Macabre said. "Come along, then," she walked and the others followed with her. Just as they were making their way past the Fairy Godmother, she grabbed Jane's arm.

"Jane," she said, her grip tightening.

"What do you want?" Jane grunted by the old thing's surprising strength. The woman held out her other hand in a fist and opened it. Jane looked and saw a compass.

"Take," the Fairy Godmother said.

Jane did, but the Godmother did not let go. She looked at it and saw that there were no cardinal points on it. There were no markings of any kind, in fact. Just an arrow in a circle made of tin and glass. "Will this show me the way to the Fear King's castle?"

"Not *want* to go," the Fairy Godmother shook her head. "*Need* to go."

"Is that it?" Jane asked, impatiently looking at the woman's arm.

"No. Beware of yourself," the Fairy Godmother spoke in an ominous tone. She let go of her arm.

"Thanks," she said, looking at the compass and rubbing her arm. "How did you know my-" she began to ask, but when she looked up, the Fairy Godmother was nowhere to be found. She glanced to her right then left and the Market began about its business as usual.

"Jane?" Mrs. Macabre asked behind her. "Are you coming?" They were several feet away from her and Jane was left in the pouring rain.

"Where did that woman go?" She asked.

"What woman?" Catie said with furrowed brows.

"The Fairy Godmother. She gave me this," she held up the compass. They all looked at each other in puzzlement. "You all spoke to her."

"I'm sorry, dear," Mrs. Macabre said. "But the only people that I've spoken to are a few vendors. Rude ones, at that. I'm sure we can find our way to the Jungle without any of *their* help," the witch paused for a moment. "In fact, the way there just popped into my mind! Strange how you can know directions to somewhere you've never been."

Jane was baffled by how they couldn't remember the strange creature, but she thought that she would worry about it later. She was far more concerned with finding the Fear King than whatever crazy old lady had to say. She placed the compass inside one of her pockets and, as if on cue, the rain stopped.

3.
THE EYES OF
THE BASILISK

The jungle was like a giant curved wall that stretched high above and from both left and right as far as they could see. Spiraling for who knows how many miles, around the Fear King's castle. Its dark towers and spires just barely peeking out from the foliage. Unlike the jungles in the Real World, this rainforest was colored in deep purples, violets, and blues, giving it an ominous, yet beautiful atmosphere in the eternal overcast that gave the days a hint of melancholy in the Hallowland.

"Well, this jungle isn't going to explore itself!" Mrs. Macabre said, turning her cane into a machete with a flick of her wrist. "Ready, loves?"

"Ready!" They all cried, though Jane hoped no one had noticed the slight tremble in her voice. With that, they all followed Mrs. Macabre as she hacked and slashed her way through the vines and entered the legendary Nightmare Jungle. Once inside, it was as if twilight was upon them. Thin beams of sunlight came shooting down from the canopies of the trees, creating dim pathways for them to follow. All the way they heard the strange, unnerving sounds of the flora and fauna around them. Jane looked down and noticed several flowers gazing up at her. Quite literally, in fact, for they each had a single eyeball in the middle of their buds.

"What are these, Mrs. Macabre?" She asked, pointing to them.

"Oh, those are eyerises, my dear," the witch chuckled, looking back at them. "Aren't they adorable?"

At first, Jane was severely unsettled by the group of flowers staring at the party, but after a few moments, she decided that they did indeed have their charms. Like most things in the Hallowland, the beauty of the world was not always evident to you immediately. They continued to march when they found a sign several feet in front of them. A plank had been nailed to a tree with white letters scrawled on it that warned: I'D TURN BACK IF I WERE YOU.

"Subtle," Arachne said, catching a flying insect in front of her and eating it.

They came onto another sign after it. BEWARE THE EYES OF THE BASILISK it read.

"Uh-oh," Bram said.

"What's wrong?" Jane asked, a knot forming in her stomach.

"A Basilisk is a serpent that can kill you if you look into its eyes," he adjusted his bowtie nervously.

"The key word is *if*, my dear Abraham," Mrs. Macabre said. "I hear they're quite beautiful creatures despite their reputation. I'm sure if we just keep our heads down and our eyes averted, we'll. . ." her words were broken by a snapping sound. She looked down and removed her boot to find that she had stepped onto what appeared to be a human femur. They all looked around and saw more bones and skulls littered here and there about the area. They also noticed that the grass was surprisingly smooth compared to the rest of the jungle. It was like someone had smoothed it out like a carpet.

Or a giant snake was using it for its' den.

"Who daressssss enter my jungle?" A soft raspy voice hissed.

"*Your* jungle?" Mrs. Macabre responded, looking all around for the source of the voice. "I thought it was the Fear King's?"

"Sssssilence!" The voice cried out in anger. "You are tressspassing and that musssst come at a pricccce."

"What price?" Jane asked in a small voice.

"The ssssame priccce that other travelerssss have paid." The voice laughed.

Mrs. Macabre gestured for them all to stay close together. As they huddled next to one another, Jane saw several leaves falling from the sky. She looked up and noticed that the branches of the trees were rustling above them. "Mrs. Macabre," she whispered. "I think it's up there." She pointed upwards.

The witch slowly looked up and nodded in agreement. "We do apologize," she said, turning her machete into a dead weasel, "but if you'll just let us pass through, we'll be on our way." An enormous reptilian tale suddenly dropped from the branches above and wrapped them all within its coils. The tail was covered in twigs, leaves, and grass, underneath which could be seen the cracked and gray color of its scales.

"You're not going anywhere," the Basilisk spoke as it wrapped its tail tighter around them.

"Blast!" Mrs. Macabre cursed as the weasel fell from her grip, rolling over next to a ribcage and turning back into her broom.

"What was that for?" Catie asked, struggling.

"Basilisks are allergic to the smell of weasels," Bram grimaced. "People used to throw them in snake holes just in case there was one down there."

"Are they allergic to bugs?" Arachne asked as the giant tail tightened around her thorax.

"Helplesssss," the Basilisk chuckled. "Helplessss as miccccccce."

"Keep your eyes shut!" Mrs. Macabre called to them. They all shut their eyes as tightly as they could.

"Do not look at me," the Basilisk warned them. "No one has gazed into my eyesssssss and lived to tell the tale." The serpent's voice was closer now in the dark, Jane could feel her head inching towards them. "Do not look at me," she repeated. Jane was struggling to breathe as the tail tightened around them. It was far more frightening to hear that cold, hissing voice in the pitch black than it was with her eyes open. What she imagined around her scared her more than the real thing. "Do not look at me," the Basilisk repeated, closer. She felt the warm breath of the snake blowing on the crown of her head. She imagined Catie, Bram, Arachne, and Mrs. Macabre's faces turning blue as the life was being squeezed out of them. "*Do not look at me,*" the voice was now right by her ear. Jane couldn't take it anymore and opened her eyes.

Staring back at her, was the most beautiful shade of green that she had ever seen. Two slits in a sea of emeralds glimmering at her with kaleidoscopic wonder, swirling, dancing, and colliding in infinite patterns and shapes. She almost wept at the sight of them, for how could something so awe-inspiring, so mesmerizing with wonder be dangerous? The Basilisk's eyes widened with terror and then, as quickly as you could snap your fingers, the eyes fled along with the rest of the serpent, up the tree from whence it came.

They all thudded on their backs, breathing heavily. "That-was-close," Catie panted.

"We're still alive!" Bram laughed with joy.

"But, I don't understand," Jane stood up as quickly as she could. "I looked into its eyes! *Hey!*" She called up the tree. "What's going on?"

"Sssssshhhh," the Basilisk's voice trembled, as if it were crying. "Go away!"

"We will not move a single step until you explain yourself!" Mrs. Macabre said, standing up and firmly placing her hands on her hips.

"You-you *looked* at me!" The Basilisk said, the branches trembling with its voice.

"I'm. . . .Sorry?" Jane said, half-apologizing and half-confused. "I couldn't help myself. I got too scared and I just had to open my eyes."

"I told you not to!"

They all looked at one another, bewildered. "I thought Basilisks can kill someone just by looking at them?" Arachne asked.

"That's what every mythology book that I've read says!" Bram said, hoping that his role as the group's monster expert hadn't come into question.

"That'sssss jussssst a myth!" The Basilisk cried. "We are so embarrasssssed by our lookssss that we let you believe it!"

"Where did all these bones come from?" Catie asked, gesturing around her.

"Travelersssss from other partsssss of the jungle," the serpent hissed. "I'm a vegetarian."

"So, you weren't going to eat us?" Jane asked, walking closer to the tree.

"I wanted to sssscare you!"

"Well. . . . Thank you. But I think your eyes are beautiful."

"You're jussssst being polite!" The Basilisk shuddered.

"No I'm not. I'm pretty bad at lying, just ask my sister."

"She is," Catie affirmed.

"You won't laugh at me if I come out?" The trees moved slightly less now.

"Promise. Right, family?" Jane looked at them and gave them a knowing look.

"Promise!" They all agreed, some easier than others.

There was a pause. The tress stopped rustling and they all momentarily began to wonder if the Basilisk and somehow vanished. Then they heard a small, "Okay. I'm coming down," from above and soon the serpent made its way down, looping itself around the tree until it was around them as it was before.

They all gasped as they stared in wonder at those beautiful green eyes. It did not matter if the rest of it had clearly seen better days- its head was just as dirty and cracked as the rest of its body was- the brilliance of its eyes made those seemingly large details very, very, small.

"*Coooool!*" Bram crowed, his own eyes growing wider.

"They're are so pretty!" Catie said with her mouth agape.

"And I thought *my* eyes were something to stare at," Arachne said, brushing four of her eight eyes with slight jealousy.

"See," Jane smiled at the giant snake, "told you you were beautiful."

"You really think sssso?" The Basilisk asked bashfully.

"Oh, yes, indeed," Mrs. Macabre stepped forward, beaming. "I've seen many creatures in my travels, but very few have such shimmering sights as you do. Here, take a look for yourself!" She reached into one of her pockets and pulled out a compact mirror. She opened it and held it up to the Basilisk, positioning it so that it could see.

At first the serpent was hesitant to look, as if its own gaze could kill itself. But it soon relented and looked into the small mirror. Its eyes grew wide like it had done before, however they were large with wonder instead of fear. Its bright green eyes never broke contact with the mirror, the jungle and our friends meant nothing to it now. It was only the hypnotic patterns that locked the Basilisk's attention. No, Jane thought, it wasn't the eyes that it was stunned by. The Basilisk was taken aback by what its eyes meant. For the first time in its life, it had seen *itself*. Really, truly seen itself. Not some horrible projection of what it thought it was, not what the myths said it looked like, but what it looked like for what it really was.

"Ooooh," the Basilisk said softly. "Oh! Oh! Oh!" She cried out and its skin began to crack even more. The leaves, twigs, and dust that had accumulated over the years of hiding from itself had fallen and underneath its old skin was a hide of green as beautiful as its eyes. The Basilisk shook off the rest of its skin from its head and looked at them without embarrassment or fear, but with love. "Thank you!" It said with fresh tears of joy in its eyes. "Thank you sssso much! What ever can I do for you?"

"Can you take us to see the Fear King?" Jane asked with excitement.

"I'm afraid I can't," the Basilisk replied apologetically. "Basiliskssss are forbidden to even come closssse to hisss casssstle. That isss why I live in the outer ring of the jungle. But I can point you in that direction!"

"That will do!" Mrs. Macabre smiled.

"Keep going north, then stop at the cube sssshaped rock."

"You've helped us more than you know!" Jane ran over to the Basilisk and hugged its tail.

"No, you have helped *me* more than you know, my child," the serpent bowed its head and licked Jane's cheek with its forked tongue. It did the same to the others. Arachne did her best to pretend it did not bother her. "Farewell, my new found friendsssss!" The Basilisk said with glee and slithered away through the jungle and out of their sight.

Though they had managed to travel quite a bit of distance after their encounter with the Basilisk, our friends did not make it to the curiously cubed shaped rock by nightfall. Instead, they decided to set up camp on a small patch by a purple toadstool.

"But, Mrs. Macabre," Catie said. "We don't have any camping equipment. How are we going to set up a tent?" She looked around, trying to find some semblance of shelter nearby, but none was to be found.

"Very observant of you, my dear Catherine," Mrs. Macabre gave her a knowing smile. She held her walking stick high up into the air and slammed it into the jungle floor, as if she was staking her territory. She stepped back and, after a few moments, the stick seemed to grow multiple legs like an insect. The legs formed a pyramid type structure and a black tarp unfolded from them. Soon they were all looking at a wholly formed tent.

"Magic. Duh." Catie laughed and smacked herself on the forehead.

Mrs. Macabre lifted up the flap of the entrance and beckoned them. "Come on in! There's plenty of room!" She quickly darted into the tent. The explorers looked at one another, not quite understanding how they could all fit inside such a small thing. But they shrugged and followed the witch, anyway.

Once they had gone through the opening they all gasped as they entered the foyer of the manor. Behind them, sat the tent that was in the jungle before, as if it had appeared from thin air. Jane and Bram lifted up the flap and saw the jungle outside. They realized that the tent was both outside the jungle and inside the manor at the same time.

"Best camping trip ever," Jane smiled at him and they went to join their friends for dinner and a good night's sleep

4.
LAUGH, CLOWN, LAUGH

The next morning, after they had all eaten a hardy breakfast, they packed up once again and continued their journey. Jane was thankful that it wasn't raining like the day before and the trees seemed to clear out a little, letting the daylight shine through the gray sky, the hazy image of the moon hung overhead as it always did in the Hallowland. She wiped her brow and was surprised by how humid the jungle seemed to get the more they walked. The sounds of the animals and strange plant life no longer seemed threatening to her. Two-headed lizards crawled down trees as three-eyed toucans flew above their heads. It was like being on the strangest safari ever.

"I think we found it," Bram suddenly said and Jane's gaze was directed from the sky to what was in front of them. The rock was just as the Basilisk said, it was a huge cubed shaped boulder that sat on a pile of smaller rocks as support. On the side of it was a bizarre arm made of stone.

"Hmmm," Mrs. Macabre said, scratching her chin. "I wonder how this gets us to the castle." They all inspected it, trying to find some sort of rune or secret message that could lead the way. The Gracey twins were near the side when Catie accidentally bumped into the arm, making it move.

"I think it's a. . . . a crank?" Catie wondered aloud.

"Let's push it together," Jane said and they both began to turn the giant arm. As the crunch of stone against stone bellowed out of the cube, something else came up deep from within the rock that made them all jump in surprise. It sounded like music from a circus.

"Go on, loves," Mrs. Macabre encouraged them to continue. They all stared at the thing with wonder and bewilderment. The twins continued to turn the arm and the music played on. The children soon realized that the tune that emerged from the cube was *Pop Goes the Weasel* and they all nearly laughed at the absurdity of it all. As the song was coming to an end, the top of the cube burst open with a huge BANG!

A giant clown head on a metal coil spring bounced up and down in the air. It had white gloved hands on metal arms attached to its sides. They all jumped back in alarm, Mrs. Macabre and Arachne positioning themselves in front of the children.

"WHO OPENED MY BOX? YUK-YUK-YUK!" The giant head asked in a loud, shuddering voice, as if it were on the verge of laughing or crying.

"I-I did," Jane stuttered, quickly glancing at Catie who gave her a stern look.

The clown head stopped bouncing and swayed slowly back and forth. "THEN YOU GET TO SEE THE GREATEST SHOW IN THE WORLD! YUK-YUK-YUK!" The head swayed menacingly, closer with every second, the head's smile growing wider and wider. It them grabbed Jane with one of its hands and, as she screamed, threw her up into the trees.

"JANE!" She heard them all cry out to her below, but that was soon drowned out by shrieks, whoops, and laughter. The twilight was nearly invisible in the trees as shadowy hands grabbed her, tossing her from tree to tree. She could not see who was grabbing her, but she assumed that from the laughing, tittering, and shapes that followed her, she was being thrown around by a pack of wild monkeys. Though, it was indeed the most alien pack of monkeys she had ever seen because their hands were not furry or coarse, but soft and smooth like silk.

Her vision tossed and turned and her ears were filled with wild, maddening shrieks until she was let go of and fell. She braced herself to hit the ground, but instead she hit some meshy material and bounced up and down, up and down. She looked and saw that she had fallen onto a trampoline. Lights hung on strings above her and she soon realized that the jungle, or at least this part of the jungle, was covered by a huge black and white circus tent.

There was one final bounce on the trampoline and then she landed on her backside which caused all the clowns in the tent to laugh hysterically. They did not look like the clowns of her times- there were none of any rainbow colored hair or enormous shoes- these clowns looked like those of another era. They were all dressed in black and white satin, each of them had creamy white faces with dark make-up around their eyes and mouths. Some of them had hats, but most of them were bald. Jane noticed something peculiar as well, they could not form words. They could laugh, that was for certain, but no words of any language came out of their throats. It appeared that they could only make the strange monkey hollering that she had heard in the trees above.

One of the clowns quickly grabbed her by the arm with a white glove and lead her to a bench near the edge of the tent. The clown motioned for her to sit, grinning at her from ear to ear, as if hooks kept his mouth from any other expression except for smiling. She did as she was told, not wanting to disturb them, she had always found clowns to be creepy, so she did not want to invoke any type of aggravation. The clown went to the center of the tent and stretched out his arms in a gesture that seemed to announce something, then another clown stepped up and smacked him in the face with a whipped-cream pie. The other clowns laughed wildly once again, but Jane failed to see the humor in it. She applauded them, nonetheless. The clowns looked at one another with concern.

The pie-covered clown walked out of the spotlight with his head down in embarrassment. One of his siblings replaced him. She held in her hand a glass of water, which she quickly drank. She then gargled the water and swallowed. Sunflowers then sprouted out of both of her ears. Though the magic trick was impressive, Jane repeated as she had done before and clapped. The clown stomped her foot and frowned in annoyance, leaving the spotlight in a silent huff.

Another clown replaced her and dropped a banana peel in front of him. He then walked back off to the side and entered once again, silently whistling as if he were on a stroll. Not looking where he was going, he slipped on the banana peel and landed backwards, his head hitting the hard floor. Cartoon birds chirped and flew around his head. Jane could relate to the pain the clown felt when she had fallen off of the trampoline, but she could only muster a small empathetic smile.

The clown got up from the floor and slapped himself on the forehead with frustration. Instead of waiting for him to get off of the stage, another female clown ran and pushed him out of the way. Eager to show off, she did a tap dance and sang a song through a kazoo. This only confused Jane even more than she already was to the point of this little revue.

Other clowns soon showcased their acts. One clown juggled five rubber chickens in the air. Another rode a unicycle. A set of identical clown twins took turns bonking one another on the head with a mallet. The next clown blew bubbles out of his nose. On and on it went, each one failing as much as the previous, until all the clowns grew so angry with one another that they piled on each other in an enormous fight.

"*Stop!*" Jane cried out to them. It had felt like she had been there for hours and her increasing boredom and worry over where her friends were got the best of her. The clown mob stopped and looked at her, all of them tied together in balloon animal knots. "Are you all trying to make me laugh?" The clowns untangled one another and formed a single file, as if a drill sergeant had called for their attention. They smiled happily. "Well, I don't know how to tell you this," she said, trying to choose her words carefully. "But I. . . I just don't think these jokes are funny."

The clowns immediately dropped to the ground crying. They sobbed in silent wails, tears streaming down their cheeks, smearing their pancake make-up. Jane had never seen a clown cry, much less a group of them, and it was far from pleasant. To see this pack of failed comedians silently bawling filled her with both pity and unnerving dread.

"Oh, I didn't mean to upset you," she said in a voice of half-concern and half-nervousness. She cautiously made her way towards the crying clowns. "It's okay. Can you explain to me what you want?" Jane patted one on the shoulder.

The clown responded by mimicking laughter, clutching his belly. He then made a sweeping gesture with his arm as if to communicate that it was non-existent.

"Have you tried being something other than funny?" She asked. The clowns responded by scratching their chins, shrugging, or shaking their heads in despair. "Well," Jane thought aloud, "you're in the Nightmare Jungle, so have you considered that what you should be doing is being scary?"

They all looked at her with just as much confusion and bewilderment as she had watching their failed comic acts. "Just try it," she encouraged them. "My friend Mrs. Macabre, says that real failure is not trying at all. So go ahead! Give it a shot!"

The clowns stared blankly at one another, until a female clown gripped the ends of her mouth and pulled. The skin stretched like taffy, making her face look like it was melting as it sunk to the floor. Jane cried out in genuine shock. "That's, uh, that's good," she said, keeping it together. "Now your turn!" She pointed to one of the troupe.

The clown thought for a moment, then snapped his fingers as if he just had an idea. He held his head and unscrewed it, turning it around and around until it popped off of his body. He then rolled his head across his arms and his shoulders like it was a ball.

"That's creepy!" She smiled. "Who's next?"

Another clown reached into their mouth and pulled themself inside out, revealing rainbow colored guts.

The twin clowns cut themselves into pieces with a chainsaw, then reassembled one another.

The banana peel clown turned himself into a large bat, keeping his black and white painted head on his body.

Soon the entire tent was filled with clown-shaped terrors. The monkey-laughing that had once filled it was now a cacophonous cry of screams. Jane was indeed frightened by how menacing the shapes were, and hoped she would not have nightmares of her own about them later, but something couldn't help her from smiling. A feeling of joy filled her amongst the horrors that transgressed in front of her. The same joy that came with seeing the Basilisk shed its skin. The joy of seeing someone finally embrace who they truly were.

All of a sudden, Mrs. Macabre, Catie Bram, and Arachne came running into the tent. "There she is!" Arachne cried, pointing to Jane, ready to fight whatever came at her.

"We've been running for so long!" Bram said, out of breath.

"These things were screaming so loud, we finally found you!" Catie shouted, relieved, yet taken aback by the sight.

"It appears we've arrived in the nick of time, my loves!" Mrs. Macabre said triumphantly, turning her cane back into her broom and guarding herself with it. "Unhand her you fiends or I'll-"

"Wait!" Jane shouted, placing herself between them and the clowns. "They aren't hurting me!"

"Not hurting you *yet*, you mean," Catie said, pointing to a clown that had just contorted himself into a Tyrannosaurus.

"I can explain," Jane pleaded and so she did. She proceeded to tell them the entire strange and harrowing journey that she had just been on. Describing every comedic act with the same results from this crowd as it was for her. Her friends reacted with pity as she recounted the weeping of the clowns then smiles grew on their faces as she explained why they appeared so threatening.

"Ghoulish gracious!" Mrs. Macabre said to the troupe. "We owe you all a tremendous apology for coming in so hot like that!" The clowns turned back into their original forms and bowed to her in solidarity.

"It's getting dark outside," Catie said. "We should get going!"

The clowns frowned and ran to Jane, hugging her and patting her on the back with appreciation as they made their way out of the tent. "You are all so sweet!" Jane giggled as one of the female clowns gave her a big wet kiss on the forehead. "Do you happen to know which way the Fear King's castle is?"

They all stopped and looked at her with large, nervous eyes, just as the sellers of the Morbid Market did. "I know it has a reputation," she said, understanding the sudden shift in mood. "But we need to get to it. He can do something that will help me like I helped you." One of the clowns stepped forward frowning with sadness. He knelt down to her and pointed towards a direction. "East!" Jane said with excitement. "Thank you so-" but the clown placed a gloved finger to his lips. He pointed in the direction again then shook his head. He then pointed to his chest and nodded slowly.

As they waved goodbye to the clowns peeking out of the huge tent against the dimming light, Jane felt confused by the clown's message, not being able to interpret it. But that soon went out of her like the daylight as she thought back to the Basilisk. It occurred to her that this adventure might be easier than she had thought.

5.
BED BUGS

The next day, the humidity of the jungle was stifling. A disgusting, sticky warmth hung over them like hot wool as they trekked deeper into the spiral. The Gracey twins were reminded of summer trips to one of their uncles' house in Louisiana, but even worse. Bram waxed poetically about his childhood in Miami, slinging his coat over his shoulder and loosening his bow tie, strolling through the jungle as if it were a fine spring morning. Mrs. Macabre shared a canteen filled with swamp water that would never run empty. Arachne would periodically shoot webbing, making a fan out of it and swishing it in front of her face until it was nothing but stringy tatters.

"Can we-please-rest," Jane panted, her tongue nearly hanging out of her mouth like a dog.

"This is nothing," Bram teased. "Y'all need to stand outside in line at Disney World in July. Now *that* is-"

"Bram, I love you," Catiie said, trying to swallow what little saliva she had, "but if you say one more word, I'm going to sing the Small World song fifty times in a row."

"Wait," Mrs. Macabre held up a hand sternly. They all stopped and looked at what was in front of them. Various beds of all shapes and sizes were placed throughout the patch of jungle. Some were on the ground, others were in trees. Round beds, long beds, short beds, bunk beds. Mattresses with no covering sat next to a gorgeous king-sized bed with ornate wood paneling that reminded Catie of the glass bed she slept in while she stayed at the Castle of the North. Though it was a surreal sight for certain, the strangest detail about it was that each bed was lined with some sort of sticky substance, as if sap were oozing from the beds themselves.

"What are they?" Jane asked, nearly falling over.

"Bed bug hives," Arachne said cautiously. "We have to be very careful."

"They look so comfy, though," Jane limped to the closest bed, a fluffy thing with a golden metal backboard. "I just need to take a break for a bit," she yawned.

"Jane don't!" Mrs. Macabre called to her. A part of Jane wanted to heed the witch's warning, but they had been walking for so long and it was so dreadfully humid out, who knew when they would set up camp again?

She flopped herself onto the bed and smiled at the softness of the goose feather pillows and the puffy mattress underneath her. She didn't even mind some of the sap sticking to her hair. It was like laying on one of the big gray clouds above her. The bed was so comfy and so delightful, that she barely even noticed the sound coming from beneath it. The hum was far away, like a chorus of voices trying to drift her off to sleep. Then it grew louder, the chorus rising and rising, until it wasn't a chorus as all.

It was the buzzing of insects.

Jane was lifted up from the bed by Catie, the sap pulling briefly from her hair and soon letting go of it. Her fantasy went as quickly off the bed as she was and reality struck in the face like a hard slap. Bugs the size of cats of black and red coloring with ten legs and wings like wasps were making their way out from underneath the beds. Talon sharp stingers poked out from the ends of their bodies.

"Okay, so they're bugs," Jane said as calmly as she could. "So what?"

"If they sting us, they're venom makes you itch for hours," Mrs. Macabre moved closer to her friends, keeping an eye on the swarm around them.

"That doesn't seem so bad," Jane shrugged.

"It isn't until you scratch your own skin off and they eat what's left," Arachne shot back at her with concern.

Jane's heart began to beat faster. *Get out!* A voice shouted inside her mind. The jungle began to grow narrower, forming a tunnel of vines and trees.

Get out! The voice shrieked louder.

She watched Mrs. Macabre try to fend off the bed bugs by shooting jets of water from her broom. Arachne strategically slung webbing at them, but the insects were too crafty and quick for them *Get out!* The voice said louder, as if it was right in front of her face. The buzzing of the bed bugs dropped from her ears, as did the calls of her name from Bram and Catie, as she stood as still as the tree the two of them were taking shelter behind.

GET OUT! The voice screamed.

Her feet ran as fast as she could. The jungle zipped by her in a blur. She felt nothing only the beating of her heart as it thundered inside her chest. She heard nothing only the sound of the air pumping in and out of her lungs. She had no sense of where she was going, no path, no destination in mind. There was only one goal, one purpose in life, and that was ro run as fast as she could, as hard as she could, for as long as she could.

Her marathon stopped when her shoe caught itself on a root and her face met the ground in an instant. She lifted her head up slowly, her forehead throbbing, her vision widening and becoming more focused. The tunnel unfolded itself and it became the jungle once again. Her heart slowed, her breathing came out of her mouth in long streams, instead of bursts of air. Then, a word came to her.

Compass.

It was the same voice as it was minutes before, but much softer, almost a whisper now. Yes, of course! The compass that the Fairy Godmother gave to her, surely it would show her the right direction. Jane quickly brushed the dirt off her hands and fumbled in her pockets. She pulled out the device that had no markings on it and saw the needle was pointing south.

She looked back and heard the far off buzzing of the bed bugs. No, that couldn't have been right. Why would it want her to go back there? She shook the compass, hoping it was only an error on her part. The needle stayed in the same direction. "Stupid, stupid, stupid!" Jane pounded her fist onto the ground. What kind of a magic compass sends you where you *don't* want to go?

She thought long and hard until the Fairy Godmother's words came back to her. *Not want. Need to go*, she had said. A cry from Catie shot through the jungle like a whip crack and Jane spun her head back into that direction again.

"Okay, okay," she whispered. "You can do this. You *need* to go back," she remained on the ground. "You *need* to go back!" She said, louder, her legs only moved an inch. She took in a deep breath and, with the roar of a lion, she screamed "YOU NEED TO BACK!"

She shot up from the ground and her feet took her back to where the insects were. As she ran, she noticed that the buzzing had stopped, but had been replaced by the low murmuring of voices. When she arrived, she saw the bugs had returned back to their hives, the beds covered with water from Mrs. Macabre's broom. She then saw Bram, Arachne, and Mrs. Macabre huddled around Catie's unconscious body.

The side of her neck was swollen and red.

Amongst her friends gathering around her sister, Jane had a memory flash in her mind of when she saved Catie from a giant squid several weeks ago. At the time, she had thought about how lucky it was that she had been there to save her. But now as she stared at the wound in Catie's neck, the patch of skin becoming more infected with every passing moment, she had thought that maybe it would have been best if she wasn't there at all.

When they both drank a potion to hide themselves from a ballroom of vampires, hers wore off first, putting them in grave danger. Maybe it would have been best if she wasn't there at all.

When they were tasked to get rid of an infestation of gremlins, Catie had been far better at it than Jane, and less prone to getting hurt. Maybe it would have been best if she wasn't there at all.

She thought about how Catie had to worry about her panic attacks. Maybe it would have been best if she wasn't there at all.

As fate or luck would have it, depending on your choice, Catie was saved by a spell cast by Mrs. Macabre just as Jane arrived on the spot. But only just. While Catie was released from the agony of itching her own skin off, she was not saved by the infection of the bed bugs' stingers. The spell placed her in indefinite sleep to slow down the venom coursing through her veins. There was no natural remedy in the Hallowland for such poison and it seemed that the only one who could cure her would be the Fear King himself. That was still miles and miles ahead of them. The young girl would be kept in her bed at the manor, in the meantime.

Jane could not sleep a wink that night. She sat on the side of her bed in the copy of the Gracey sisters' room. She watched her sister, now with a sticky remedy covering her wound on her neck. It reminded Jane of the strange substance that Mrs. Macabre had used to heal her leg after she had been pierced by the barbed-back of a gremlin. Catie had saved her then. Now it was time for Jane to return the favor.

The voices of her friends danced around in her mind.

"It's not your fault!" Bram had said.

"You were scared!" Arachne tried to console her as the tears ran down Jane's face. "Everyone gets scared!"

"There's nothing you could have done, my dear," Mrs. Macabre had given her a sympathetic smile and a kind hand on her shoulder.

But the words from outside of herself paled in comparison to the ones that soon replaced them from the inside of herself. *How could you have ran away like that!* One of them shouted. *Your sister! Your own sister!* Another voice chimed in. *You're nothing but a coward!* That one sounded like Courtney

Clearwater. *If you had just sucked it up and gotten a grip on yourself then this whole thing wouldn't have happened!*

It's strange what voices we decide to listen to and which ones we do not. All the praise, all the accolades, all the words of affection can be showered onto to us for a million years, but when we hear a single form of shame, embarrassment or anger, the entire house of cards collapses. Our feet of bronze turns to clay. Our metal armor crumples in on itself as if it were made of paper. Nothing positive that anyone can say to us can compete with the power of the horrible things we say to ourselves. They wipe them from our mind like the tide washing away a beautiful sandcastle. We may spend our entire lives learning how to love ourselves, but fear is always there. Waiting in the dark.

Jane had written a note to them all explaining what she must do. She told them not to worry, though she knew that would be impossible. She told them that it was her desire to see the Fear King and it should be her responsibility to see it through alone. It was clear that she had put them all, let alone her sister, in life threatening danger. Who knows what lurked at the heart of the jungle. She promised them that once the Fear King had cured her of her anxiety, she would return with his help for Catie. She left the note in an envelope on her pillow.

She then grabbed a backpack from her closet and, after kissing Catie on the forehead, she made her way down to the foyer. It was eerie being in the manor this late at night. She had always found her own home to be a little creepy at night, but this one had even more of an air of forbidding to it. During the day, the candles had been lit and the manor had a warm magic to it. The manor felt alive and full of wonder. But now with all the candles snuffed out, it felt more like a haunted house than ever. The walls and ceiling creaked as if it were breathing, the cobwebs drifted softly within the cool air. The ticking of clocks whispered down the halls like tiny heartbeats.

Jane had packed enough food and drink to last her three days. She had gone to the kitchen and picked out a jar of banshee berries and filled a thermos with swamp water. With one last look at the silent dark foyer of the manor, she opened the flap of the tent and was back in the Nightmare Jungle.

It felt even more endless in the dark. Jane thought that she could get lost in any direction, like flying into outer space, and never find her way out of it. She reached into her pack and pulled out a small lantern that she had found in a cupboard in the foyer. She took out a match from a small box and lit it. The yellow amber glow gave her surroundings a small bit of comfort. She saw bugs that were shaped like spirals moving up trees and the rustling of all sorts of creatures above and far off in the distance. She pulled out the Fairy Godmother's compass and trusted it to show her where she needed to go.

6.
THE TERRIBLE TEACHINGS OF MS. RABIES

Jane had been able to get at least a couple of hours of sleep before morning. As she used her backpack for a pillow, her dreams were not solid events as they usually were, but fluid. Strange images and sounds she could not make out slipped through her unconsciousness like water. When she awoke, she did not know how to feel about them- a mix of unease and confusion knotted inside of her gut. She chalked it up to it being the atmosphere of the Nightmare Jungle itself as the main cause. It had seemed that the environment scrambled ones subconscious when asleep.

After a quick breakfast of banshee berries, she pulled out the Fairy Godmother's compass. As she walked her way through the dense foliage of trees and vines, the compass guided her left and right. She noticed that the humidity was getting stronger the deeper she went, now feeling more like a sauna than ever. But she kept herself hydrated with the swamp water, taking tiny sips here and there, which kept her cool and most importantly moving.

She was headed east when she heard a sound unlike any other that she had heard in the jungle until that point. At first, she thought it was the calling of some resident nightmare-bird, but as she listened closely, she realized it was the ringing of a bell. It was low and loud, echoing through the jungle in a way that reminded her of the church bell that would ring in movies about small towns. She looked at the compass and saw that the needle was changing its direction with every chime of the bell. Slowly it moved from right, all the way to the left side of the device pointing west, towards the source of the bell. Jane shrugged and thought that if the compass had given her the courage to go back and try to help her friends, then it probably had her best intentions at heart.

After going several yards in that direction, she stumbled upon not a church, but a schoolhouse. It looked brand new, painted pearl while with a dark slated roof. It looked like the single room schools that used to be in fashion a couple of centuries before she was born. Jane had seen paintings of them in her history books, but she couldn't help but feel a small sense of amazement as she walked towards it. Here it was, right in front of her, in a jungle of all places. The Hallowland kept getting stranger and stranger.

The front door of the schoolhouse was open and as she walked in, she saw sitting in rows of desks, were children. She could not see their faces because they were all facing the blackboard at the end of the large room, but they were dressed in period accurate clothing, as if they had all stepped out of the history books. The masculine students mostly wore suspenders, white button shirts and pants with their hair neatly combed back. Whereas the feminine students wore plaid dresses and kept their hair braided in pigtails.

"Excuse me," she tapped one of them on the shoulder. "Do you know where your teacher is? I was hoping they could help me find someplace." The student said nothing, continuing to stare at the blackboard. The head never moved.

Jane went to another student, this time standing in front of them so that they could see her. "Excuse me-" she began, but never finished because the student's head turned to the right, hiding their face. Jane walked over to the right, but the head moved to the left. She went in all sorts of directions, each time the head would spin in the opposite direction. In fact, all the students' heads would do so. Whenever Jane would try and meet their gaze, their heads would turn and hide their faces, never uttering a word.

"Fine," she huffed, frustrated and found an empty desk in the back. She sat there for what seemed like thirty minutes. None of the students looked or talked to one another, they all stared at the large oak desk in front of the blackboard at the end of the room. The bell continued to chime. Jane glanced at the clock on the wall and it ticked along with the bell. Waiting and waiting and waiting and-

"Good morning, children," a voice said from the end of the room. If you had mistaken the old woman standing in front of the desk for a bird, you would not have been taken for a fool. Her back was arched in a way that forced her neck to stick out and peer down at you, as if she were perched on a branch of a tree. Her hair sat upon her head like a nest of white curly webbing. The nails on her fingers were quite long and could easily snatch a helpless mouse running from its predator or grab an unsuspecting fish from a river. Even her old dress was covered in feather patterns, and her black heels dug into the

wood of the schoolhouse like talons. Her eyes were large and glared out from underneath her small glasses which sat on her beak of a nose with the intensity of a hawk.

"Good morning, Ms. Rabies," the children responded in a cold, droning tone that made Jane think of ice sliding in a glass. She was shocked by how little variety there was in the voices. They were merely repeating the same voice.

"We have a new student joining us," Ms. Rabies gestured to Jane with her claws. "Please welcome Jane Gracey, class."

"Hello, Jane Gracey," all of the students turned their heads and Jane was forced to repress a scream. The faces, which she had finally glimpsed, were not faces at all. They had no eyes, no noses, or mouths. They were merely heads of smooth skin staring back at her.

A shriek pierced through the air, making Jane grit her teeth and cover her ears. Ms. Rabies was using one of her claws to write on the blackboard. As the scream continued, so did her writing, until it finally said it white lightning bolt letters: JANE GRACEY.

"Now," Ms. Rabies turned around and paced the length of the desk, her hands clasped behind her. "Which of you can tell me what Jane is afraid of?"

"I can! I can!" Shouted a faceless student with one of their hands raised high.

"Yes?" Ms. Rabies asked politely.

"She's afraid of her sister dying!" The student said proudly.

"Good, good," Mrs. Rabies nodded. "Anyone else?"

"Me!" Another student bolted their hand up.

"Go on, then."

"She's afraid of being afraid!"

"Excellent," Ms. Rabies smiled sharp yellow teeth at the student. "Who else would like to have a go?"

"Um, Ms. Rabies?" Jane asked, sheepishly, her palms sweating. "Can you just tell me where the Fear King's castle-"

"QUIET!" Ms. Rabies screamed at her, sounding more like a bird than ever. "YOU WILL SPEAK ONLY WHEN YOU HAVE BEEN CALLED UPON. IS THAT UNDERSTOOD?"

"Ye-yes, ma'am," Jane recoiled in her seat, shocked by the fury that erupted from this horrible old woman. The rest of the class tittered.

"Now class," Ms. Rabies proceeded in an even tone. "Can you tell me *why* Jane is afraid of those things?"

There was a moment of silence, as if the students were considering the question. Jane's body stiffened, anticipating the answer like a helpless prisoner awaiting execution. Finally a student responded.

"Because. . . she's always felt responsible for her sister?" They said in a tone that suggested apprehension.

"Well done!" Ms. Rabies commended the child, who then gave out a small sigh of relief. "Can anyone tell me why Jane is afraid of being afraid?"

A student stood up from his seat. "Because she thinks being afraid is the same thing as being weak!"

A fire began to burn deep inside of Jane.

"Excellent!" Ms. Rabies applauded. "On to our-"

"I've had enough of this lesson," Jane said through gritted teeth.

"WHAT DID I SAY, CHILD!" Ms. Rabies roared, making the schoolhouse shake. "I SAID YOU WILL SPEAK ONLY WHEN-"

"I heard what you said," Jane stood up with her fists clenched. "And I think you're a very bad teacher!"

"WHAT?" Ms. Rabies' face turned the color of red hot coals. "HOW DARE YOU SPEAK TO ME THAT WAY YOU LITTLE URCHIN!" Her body grew and took the form of an enormous vulture. "YOU INSIGNIFICANT LITTLE WORM!"

"I'm not afraid of you!" Jane screamed back at her with all the courage she could muster..

"YOU WILL BE!" Ms. Rabies grinned at her. "MY CHILDREN FIND THE TASTE OF FEAR TO BE MOST SATISFYING!"

The schoolhouse rumbled as tree branches burst out of the floorboards, taking the schoolhouse, the desks, and the students with it. Jane grabbed onto the nearest branch as it soared up and up until she could see the spires of the Fear King's castle still miles off. The schoolhouse itself had been turned into a large nest and the students resembled baby vultures as well. Their faceless visages were now replaced with mouths filled with sharp teeth. Their jaws snapped and their tongues licked their lips with hunger towards her.

"NOW YOU WILL LEARN YOUR LESSON," the huge Ms. Rabies said as she carried Jane above the nest with her talons clinging onto the backpack. "YOU WILL LEARN WHAT HAPPENS WHEN YOU DISRESPECT YOUR TEACHER!"

Jane let out a scream as she twisted this way and that, trying to get away. Ms. Rabies wings beat with such a force that Jane's hair was constantly blowing across her vision. "SCREAM ALL YOU WANT, GIRL! SCREAMING MAKES THE MEAT TENDER!" Ms. Rabies cackled. The tiny mouths of her children bobbed up and down, just barely scraping Jane's shoes.

Jane heard a tearing sound from behind her and she plummeted down past the nest. She had the wind knocked out of her as she struck a branch and fell down forever until she landed on the ground with a thud. The contents of her backpack fell around her like broken toys. She heard a screech of fury from Ms. Rabies high above when everything went dark.

7.
OPERATION

She felt cold. It felt like she was laid out on something that was crafted somewhere between a bed and a table. Her eyes slowly opened to see large orbs of light that circled above her. As her vision grew clearer, she realized that the orbs of light were coming from a an old light fixture that hung from the ceiling. She also saw that she was in a stadium like theatre, lined with white tiles. Shadows moved above the tiles, shifting and talking to one another, as if they were waiting for something to happen. She looked down and saw that she was sprawled across an operating table.

"Ah! You're awake!" Said a voice next to her. Jane turned her head slowly to see that the owner of the voice was a tall man wearing an old style surgeon's outfit. His hands were covered in white rubber gloves that squeaked with every movement and the bottom half of his face was disguised by a cloth mask that wrapped around his ears. The curious thing about him, however, were the black pupils that gazed at her through yellow eyes. It reminded her of the eyes of a panther.

"Where-where am I?" She asked, finding her voice.

"You're with the Good Doctor, of course!" He said proudly. The shadows above him chuckled. "It's a good thing

I found you before that nasty old bird could snatch you back up!"

"I have to go," Jane tried to get up from the operating table. "I have to get to the Fear King's castle! I have to find a way to-"

"Now, now," the Good Doctor said, pushing her back onto the table with an intensity that surprised her. "We can worry all about that once the procedure is over. Doctor's orders!" He wagged a finger in front of her face and the shadows chuckled again.

"Procedure? What procedure? Did I break something when I fell?" She tried to mentally scan her body but found no evidence of a broken bone.

"Oh, no," the Good Doctor said. "I'm not *that* kind of doctor. I'm the kind of doctor that likes to see *inside* of people. I like to poke, prod, wiggle around inside of folks to see what makes them tick." He walked over off to the side, his feet echoing against the tiles, and rolled over a small cart. He removed the cloth on top of it to reveal a single scalpel, its blade grinning back at her in the light.

"Don't I need, uh, you know. . . . anesthetic, or something?" She asked, her voice quavering.

"I'd prefer you to be awake for this procedure," the Good Doctor said, holding up the instrument. "It's the only way to know for sure if we're getting anywhere."

Her heart began to beat rapidly in her chest, but she could not move a muscle. Instead of running, her body was horribly glued to the operating table. The shadows leaned in closer to try and get a good view of the coming surgery.

"This won't hurt a bit," the Good Doctor said as he moved the scalpel towards her torso. Jane shut her eyes, bracing for a sharp unimaginable pain. But there was none. She opened her eyes again after a few moments and saw that the Good Doctor had made a long cut from her chest to her navel, but there was no blood. There was no pain at all, in fact. She saw no bones or organs inside of her peeking out through the slit in her shirt, she only saw a black void inside her. In a strange way, this made her even more nervous than she already was.

"Let's see what we've got here," the Good Doctor reached into the hole and pulled out a book she recognized instantly.

"It's the biography of Mary Shelley!" She cried out, shocked by what was inside of her.

"Your favorite author, I suppose?" The Good Doctor, asked, scratching his mask in thought.

"I've read it tons of times. Catie, my sister, always makes fun of me for re-reading it. She-"

"Boring," the Good Doctor interrupted her as he threw the book over his shoulder. It didn't

make a sound. It was as if the book had vanished into thin air. "We need to go deeper." He plunged his hand in again, going down to his elbow this time. Jane watched the shadows whisper and converse with one another.

"Who are they?" She asked quietly, afraid of what the answer might be.

"Shhhhh," the Good Doctor said. "I'm trying to concentrate," he continued to move around in the hole until he exclaimed, "ah-ha!" He pulled out the coffin box that she kept on her nightstand.

"How did you get that?" Jane asked, a cold sweat forming on her brow. This was a frightening experience to be certain, but something about the Good Doctor finding such a personal item within her chilled her to the bone.

The Good Doctor continued to ignore her as he opened the box with greedy zeal. "Movie tickets," he mumbled to himself as he pulled out a pair of paper tickets for one of her favorite movies that she saw with Catie and Bram. It was a horror film, of course, and Jane's parents had to supervise them since they were underage. But the thrill they got from seeing it had stayed with her ever since. It felt like they were looking at something that they should not be seeing. Something secret. Something forbidden, I'm sure you've felt the same way after staying up late to watch something your parents didn't approve of. And I'm sure you felt the same electricity Jane had felt.

"A piece of straw," he continued as he chucked the straw that Mrs. Macabre had given her.

"Hey!" Jane called to him, annoyed. "A friend gave that to me!" The way the Good Doctor casually discarded such things that meant so much to her filled her with a sick, sticky sensation. It was beyond rude, it felt downright invasive.

The Good Doctor emptied the contents of the box and threw it on the ground. He sighed in a way that suggested to her a deep sense of frustration. "Time to get serious," he reached over to the tray and took a device that she hadn't see before. It was so large, the Good Doctor had to use both hands to carry it. He placed it at the hole and turned a crank on it, which activated two metal plates that expanded the hole with every crank. She winced and cried out with every turn, suddenly feeling a deep piercing pain inside of her.

"Please stop!" She said through gritted teeth as tears formed in her eyes.

"*Now* we're getting somewhere!" The Good Doctor said happily. The shadows above him chuckled with equal delight. The Good Doctor placed both of his arms in the wide hole and moved them inside of her.

A memory flashed into Jane's mind. During this horrible moment of pain and confusion, she remembered the dentist's office her and Catie would go to when they were smaller. At the end of each appointment, they were allowed to choose a toy from a large plastic treasure chest. They would dig around, searching for any sign of a monster doll or a set of fake vampire teeth, but they more often than not left with just a kazoo or a paddle ball. That is what the Good Doctor's operation reminded her of. He was scavenging his way through the treasure chest of herself to find whatever gold he could find.

"Finally!" He cried out after several moments. "For a second there, I thought all hope was lost!" He pulled out a framed photo of her, Catie, and their parents. They were on vacation in Hawaii several years prior. Their parents beamed out at her in a similar fashion as the sun and the ocean behind them did. She and Catie did the best they could to smile, but their utter contempt for such a bright place was visible in their eyes. Even the glorious rainbow seemed to mock them in the corner. Still, the fact that she was seeing her parents and her sister again in such a dreadful place filled Jane with an aching longing that pulled at every muscle in her body.

"Don't-don't do this!" She pleaded through sobs.

"Yes, yes," the Good Doctor nodded confidently. "This is very interesting progress," he placed a hand on the device, which was now a sewing machine, and turned it on. Within minutes, Jane was stitched up. Every time the needle struck her skin, it burned her more and more.

"Will you let me go?" She choked on her tears.

"Just one more thing," the Good Doctor raised a finger. He then held the picture in front of her and took out a lighter. He flicked it on and set the photo ablaze. As the faces of her family melted away in the red and blue flames, so did the invisible chains that kept her locked to the table. Terror and anguish were replaced with white hot rage as she stared into those gleeful yellow eyes.

Jane let out an enormous scream that came from deep within her and she swiped at the Good Doctor. He let out a cry as he turned, his mask falling to the floor and the flaming picture crashed onto the tiles. The shadows stood silently, awaiting to see what would happen. Jane leapt off the table and ran towards a pair of double doors at the end of the theatre, until she heard a sound.

Her shoes screeched as she stopped to hear a low purring sound from behind. She looked and saw that the Good Doctor's mask had covered a tiger-like maw, flesh colored with dark whiskers that poked off of the sides. White fangs drooled and hissed at her. The Good Doctor got on all fours and pounced at her.

Jane found her strength again and continued to run just as he was about to land on her. She was out the doors and back into the Nightmare Jungle. It was night, but she had illumination in the worst way possible. Clouds filled the sky as lightning bolts struck down from above. They clapped and speared the jungle every few seconds. *Think later, run now*, her inner-voice told her and she booked it.

Through vines and diving past trees, she went deeper and deeper into the spiral. She looked behind her and saw the Good Doctor gaining behind her through the white flashes of the storm.

""Nowhere to hide, little girl," the Good Doctor purred at her. All signs of delight were gone from his voice and instead it took the timbre of a ferocious and hungry jungle cat stalking his prey. "I'll rip you, I'll tear you, I'll feast on everything that's inside your heart. Your juicy, meaty soul smells *so delicious.*"

She went to hide behind a tree, just as the Good Doctor slashed at her, dark claws ripped through his rubber gloves, when a bolt struck the tree, setting it on fire like the photograph.

Jane was sent rocketing backwards and she saw the Good Doctor running, screaming in rage and horror at the fire. She looked around, trying to find any source of shelter that she could. She finally saw a collection of rocks that had fallen off a cliff, creating a cubby of sorts for her to crawl into. She ran in, clutching her legs in the fetal position, her heart thundering away. She thought about Mrs. Macabre, Catie, Bram, Arachne, Mrs. Mirth, and Jack Lantern. She thought about how none of this would have happened if she never left them.

She hoped that she could make it through the night.

8.
THE ABYSS

Sleep abandoned her as well as her sanity. Her head felt like a fishbowl, filled to the brim with murky liquid. The hours of the night stretched on into day so very slowly, yet so very fast. As she moved through the jungle, her mind and body were no longer one. They were separate entities, one disconnected from the other in a way that made her feel like every step she took was not of her own will. She wanted to collapse on the grassy floor, to sleep finally, but she had to keep moving.

Jane reached a clearing and she rubbed her eyes to make sure that she was seeing it correctly. It was true, right in front of her was a small pond of black glass. She could see the gloomy clouds reflected onto it, like one sky on top of the other. She pulled out the Fairy Godmother's compass and saw that the needle pointed towards a hill on the other side. She took a step forward and then stopped. She considered the last time she consulted the compass, it lead her to that horrible schoolhouse. And the time before that lead her to witness the aftermath of Catie's sting. The Fairy Godmother had told her that it was meant to take her where she needed to go, but now she wasn't so sure. In her exhausted and aggravated state, she nearly threw the thing across the way, but something stayed her hand.

She couldn't explain why she felt it, her emotions were too busy whirling around inside her head like a tornado, but somehow she felt like she had to keep holding on to it. That was the difference between needing something and wanting something, she supposed. Wanting something is because you are making a choice, needing something is because the choice has already been made for you.

Jane sighed and stomped her feet, glad that her friends could not see her in an embarrassing moment of immaturity. But she put the compass back into her pocket and pressed onward. The journey to the other side wasn't that far away, after all. She stepped onto the black glass and saw her reflection of her foot meet her real one. She was startled at first, due to her mind instinctively feeling that she should be falling into water, but she merely stayed there. She took another step forward and she was fully on top of the giant mirror. She walked briskly across it, strolling with her darker self underneath her. She was about at the halfway point when she noticed that the surface was making a soft squishy sound. She ignored it, but soon her feet got stuck. She lifted up her leg and a long trail of black ooze was hanging from her shoe, like bubble gum. Jane tried to walk some more, but every step she took got stickier and stickier.

Jane heard a sound near her like a soft wailing and looked next to her and saw black bubbles fizzing across the face of the mirror. The bubbles soon formed a mouth of tar. "*Help us*!" The mouth cried to her.

"Who?" She asked, disgusted by the sight. She noticed that her feet were beginning to sink into the mirror.

"*Us! Us! Us!*" Several faces appeared from the muck, wailing in sorrow. Their expressions were grotesque with despair.

"I-I can't!" Jane said, trying to get through as quickly as she could. As she struggled to reach the hill, she sunk lower and lower. The hard glass turning into ooze all around her.

"*We are all so very lonely!*" More faces and voices appeared in a chorus of grief. "*We who are unloved and frightened! We who long for a friend! We who only wish to be held and cared for!*" Soon sticky arms tried to grab for her with sticky fingers.

"Let go of me!" She screamed at them. She was almost there. Just a little bit farther. Just a little bit closer.

"*They all say that! They all think that they can reach the end! But we know better! We know the prison of hope! We know the freedom of giving up! Hope is for the foolish!*"

"Come on! Come on!" She snarled as her entire torso sank into the horrible swamp. Her arms groped for the ground, her head just barely above the surface.

"*There is no point in fighting it, little girl!*" The legion of woes cried out to her. "*Join us! Join us! JOIN US!*" Her face sank into the tar along with the rest of her, one single hand fell onto the other side.

The dark was suffocating. She wanted to scream, she wanted to claw, she wanted to fight her way out. But a chilling sensation overtook her like the cold chill of the swamp.

Maybe it was for the best that she wasn't going to make it.

After all, her running away from Mrs. Macabre and her friends had only gotten her into danger.

No more panic attacks.

No more putting her sister at risk.

No more bullies at school.

No more worries about what her parents would think.

No more fear.

Just. . .

Give. . .

Up. . .

As her fingers were about to sink into the muck forever, something grabbed them. It felt like tiny pin pricks. They were pulling her slowly but surely upwards. The coldness of the swamp was soon dissolved by the hot air of the jungle. She heard the moans coming out of the ooze, splashes of it raining on her face as the hands tried their best to take hold of her. Inch by inch, she was lifted out and fell onto the damp grass of the hill on the other side. Finally, Jane Gracey slept.

9.
SONG OF THE
JUNGLE

"Hey, kid!" A gruff voice called to her. "Wake up!" The accent was slightly familiar. It reminded Jane of the driver of a taxi cab that her family shared on a trip to New York. "Are ya, there?" The voice asked again.

She opened her eyes and a series of startling images met her. Firstly, she was no longer in the jungle proper, but in a long cave that had a waterfall at the end of its mouth. Secondly, she realized her clothes were wet, and that the remnants of that terrible tar were no longer to be found on her. But most startling of all was that the owner of the voice was a creature with the body of corgi and the head of a human baby. She let out a scream and crawled back away from it as quickly as she could.

"I get that a lot," the animal said, as if expecting her response.

"Get back!" Jane yelled at it, swatting it away with her arms and continuing to crawl backwards until she hit the wall of the cave.

"Easy kid, I ain't gonna hurt ya," the thing said, stepping towards her.

"You don't fool me," she snorted, thinking of all the deceptive creatures she had encountered since entering the jungle.

The animal let out a large sigh. "Fine," he rolled over on his back, exposing his belly. "Ya happy now?"

She stared at it for a moment, her nerves were so shot with adrenaline that it took her a bit to realize the thing wanted to be petted. She slowly reached out a hand and then gently began to caress the creature's belly.

"*That* hits the spot, right there!" It said as it closed its eyes and a small smile grew on its lips. Its left leg began to thump against the stone floor.

"What's your name?" Jane giggled. The animal now seemed grotesquely cute.

"Frank. What's yours?"

"Jane, What are you, exactly?"

"I'm a nightmare!" Frank said, annoyed. "Whataya think I'm doin' in the Nightmare Jungle? Takin' a vacation?"

"Sorry," she smiled at Frank's attitude, which somehow made him even cuter. Then she stopped, remembering why she was here in the first place. "Did you... Did you carry me out of that tar pit?"

"Yeah, that was me," Frank got up and shook his furry coat. "If I hadn't been lookin' for my mornin' meal, ya would've been a gonna, for sure. What's a nice girl like you swimmin' around in the Abyss, anyways?"

Now it was her turn to let out a sigh. She told Frank of her panic attacks, how she came to the Nightmare Jungle, who Mrs. Macabre was, what she wanted from the Fear King. Everything that had transpired until this moment.

"Hot crow," Frank said, shaking his head in disbelief. "You're lucky to be alive, ya know that?"

"Well, you helped out," Jane said. "Thank you, Frank. You're very kind."

"I've got my moments," Frank gave that small smile again, a little embarrassed by her compliment. His face suddenly dropped. "Wait a second . . ."

"What is it?" Jane asked, taken aback by how quickly his manner changed. It reminded her of how dogs and babies change emotions with the snap of your fingers. Which made his particular form appropriate.

"That witch lady you was tellin' me about," his eyes darted back and forth, trying to remember. "Was she with some kinda spidery lookin' chick?"

"Yes!" Jane cried out with excitement. "That's our friend Arachne!" She was not fond of how Frank described her as a *chick*, but she decided to let it slide.

"And was a boy about your age with 'em too?" He was now looking at her, certain of his suspicions.

"Bram!" A pang of longing hit Jane's heart as she said his name. She missed her found family so much.

"I saw them the other day!" Frank said, his tail now wagging. "They were almost to the Fear King's castle!"

"They were?" Her heart nearly leapt out of her chest. She was overjoyed to hear that they had made it and was not ensnared by any nightmares on their way. "Can you take me to the Fear King's castle?"

His tail stopped wagging. "Look kid," he said with apprehension. "Ya seem like ya gotta good heart and all. I feel bad for ya situation, but that may not be a good idea."

Her heart felt like it had been thrown off of the waterfall at the end of the cave. "Why not?"

"Ya see, the Fear King's a pretty dangerous guy. There's a reason why no one has seen 'im. If you thought things were scary out *there*, you haven't seen nothin' yet. Some say he *made* this jungle. Anyone who can make what's out there, including yours truly, means business."

Jane swallowed her anger and moved closer to Frank. She placed his head in her hands. "Frank," she said quietly. "I have been through *so much* since I got here. I've nearly been tortured or worse by this place. Back home, my panic attacks are ruining my life. My sister- *my only sister*, Frank- is lying asleep with bed bug venom inside of her. The only person that can help me and her is the Fear King. Even if what you said is true about him, I have to ask him for help. I've come too far not to."

Frank looked into her eyes with his own wide green ones. Almost hypnotized, like he was staring at a basilisk. "All right, kid," he finally said. "I'll take ya too 'im."

Jane kissed him multiple times on top of his bald head. "Good boy!"

"But don't say I didn't warn ya!" He wandered off into a corner filled with rags and bones. A small ramshackle bed that he had made for himself.

"What are you doing?" She asked, trying to contain her joy.

"Sleeping," he said, curling up on the bed. "Savin' your life has made me tired. I suggest you get some rest too. The castle isn't far, but ya gonna need your strength tomorrow," he closed his eyes and made himself comfortable. "Night, kid,"

"Night, Frank," she smiled, thankful that she had finally found a new friend in these dark times.

Jane was unable to sleep that night, but not because of fear or anxiety. No, her source of insomnia was driven by hope. Hope that she would finally rid herself of this curse inside of her. Hope that she would bring back some magical medicine that would wake Catie up and exorcise the venom from her body. Hope to see her friends again. Instead of a fire that lit her body awake like in the electrical storm, it was a kind of light that filled her being.

As she sat with her legs crossed behind the waterfall, watching the moonlight hit the jungle through the screen of water, she could hear Frank whimpering in his sleep. She did her best not to laugh, but it was almost impossible as she would occasionally glance behind her and see a back leg scratching his human ear as he slumbered.

She breathed out a sigh and took the compass out of her pocket again. The needle was spinning around and around, not in a frantic way, but in a slow deliberate pace. She furrowed her brows at the device and thought about how strange it was. Not to mention the strangeness of the person that gave it to her. What *was* the Fairy Godmother, anyway? Was she a real fairy as her title implied or was she something else? After all, the only person that seemed to have any recollection of her was Jane herself.

She closed her eyes and thought about her journey thus far. It had become increasingly more dangerous and dream-like as it went on. She supposed that would be the case in the Nightmare Jungle. The farther you get to the center of the spiral, the more untangled and weird reality became. Even by the Hallowland standers. She took a deep breath in and let it out. She felt the cold hard stone underneath her and felt the mist of the waterfall spraying on her face. She could hear the sounds of beast and bird alike as she breathed in and out. She could sense the insects and the reptiles crawling and slithering on the ground. She could feel the brush of every vine and every tree that swayed in the wind.

The image of the spiral returned to her. It moved around and around at a steady pace like the needle of the compass on her lap. She thought about how all the creatures, great and small moved along with the dance of the spiral. How night turned into day. How the wind blew in and out like her breathing. She thought about how the spiral may not be a spiral after all, but a wheel. A wheel that was always turning, the good and the bad, always moving at this one pace. She thought about everything in the jungle having a purpose. How each and every thing in it contributed to the wheel. The screeching and howling of the jungle turned into a symphony. An entire orchestra made of animals and plants that would continue to play until the wheel stopped turning.

Jane opened her eyes and smiled as she listened to its beautiful song.

10.
THE FEAR KING

Jane had only been able to catch a couple of hours of sleep, but nevertheless, she woke up more refreshed than she had in days. In appeared that her meditation at the waterfall had done wonders for her body. Frank had hunted several nightmare critters- a hybrid of squirrel and fox- which she promptly cooked after making a small fire. Frank thanked her for doing so, having never tried roasted nightmare fox before-only raw- and found it to be delicious. They soon headed towards their destination.

The jungle had grown denser here. So much so that Frank had to guide her through the dark with the sound of his voice. She heard the soft sounds of rolling brooks, birds screaming from above, and insects scurrying about her feet. The anxiety of survival had left her now that she had a guide and that she had a sense of connection with the jungle itself. She didn't feel that she was the jungle per se, but that she was a part of it. That everything in it was made up of the same elements that she was made up of somehow. She was not only relieved by this newfound confidence but was shocked by the deep change within her. It felt similar to when the Good Doctor had opened her up, but this time it did not feel invasive or painful. It felt like there was a whole other side of herself that opened itself up to her. Like she had just discovered a new room in a house that she had always lived in.

"Well, we've made it," Frank said, stopping at a tree. She saw the dim light of day on the other side and took several steps forward into it. She squinted, holding a hand up to the sky to shield herself from the illumination, but once she did, she wondered at all that surrounded her. They had reached the center of the spiral, the jungle now forming an open circle that stretched on for miles.

The Fear King's castle stood at the center of it, and as far as first impressions went, it had certainly seen better days. The dark stone was now a swampy green from algae and mold. The spires were crumbling, and the dragons that decorated the entire facade in gargoyle and other carved forms were decaying along with the rest of the palace. It looked to Jane as if the castle was at the bottom of a well made up of the jungle itself and would never find a way out of it. The regal nature of the structure now had a melancholic pity to it, like it was waiting to die.

"Shall we? Frank asked, walking up to her, paying no mind to the state of disrepair. They both walked up to the mighty wooden doors and Jane knocked. With just the slightest touch, the old wood of one of the doors opened with a slow mournful cry, Blackness greeted them as well as a current of cold air that gasped for freedom out of the castle and into the humidity of the jungle.

"You go first," Jane said quickly to Frank.

"Ya really *are* scared of everything," Frank chuckled and lifted his head up with a courageous flick.

"Dogs can see in the dark," she shot back at him, but he only responded with a side glance and a wry smile as he trotted in.

"You can come in," his voice echoed in the dark. "Just hope ya not allergic to dust." He let out a short sneeze.

Jane walked in carefully, tip-toeing over anything that could be in the way. She was immediately hit with a sneezing attack. After rubbing her nose and sniffing, her eyes adjusted to the dark and she saw that the outside of the castle was spotless compared to its interior. Cobwebs and dust filled the giant foyer as if it hadn't been occupied in at least a hundred years. Paintings that hung on the walls displaying the Fear King's exploits were indecipherable, some even had gapping holes in them made by rats and moths. The red velvet carpet was weathered and torn, no longer the bright crimson of its glory days, but the dull shade of blood. The chandeliers that were once gold and gleaming, were now as gray as rainclouds, Jane even had to step around one that had fallen in a desperate attempt to leave this place. A harpsichord stood in the corner, broken and unloved. Its few keys stood out of it like broken teeth.

"Anybody home?" Frank called out, his voice echoed over and over again against the walls. No response. He barked several times which made the walls shake as if they were startled.

"How are we going to find them?" Jane asked, catching up to Frank and then sneezing again.

"Bless you," a voice said from up the wide staircase in front of them. It was a man dressed in a spotless suit with a black tailcoat. His white hair was brushed slickly back on his scalp and his mustache was curled at the ends. A monocle was held by one of his thick, but finely groomed eyebrows which reflected the two candles that he held in each hand. He was the cleanest thing in the entire castle.

"Thank you," Jane said, catching herself. "Who are you?"

"My name is Mr. Both," the gentleman said. Then, without any warning, he split in half. Each side standing on one leg and carrying each candle.

"And I'm Mr. Right," said the right side.

"And I'm Mr. Left," said the left side.

"At your service," Mr. Both said as he reconnected himself.

"Cool," Jane couldn't help herself. The sight of the butler's bones and muscles peeking out from each side when he separated was delightfully gruesome.

"You must be the missing Gracey sister, yes?" Mr. Both asked, paying no mind to her remark.

"I am," she answered. "How did you know-"

"His Majesty's guests have been looking for you," he cut her off. "They have been. . . *eager* to find you," he spoke in an annoyed tone as if he had been subjected to a marathon of questions.

She and Frank both looked at each other with joy. "You mean Mrs. Macabre? And my other friends?" She asked him.

"Indeed," he sniffed. "They arrived here two days ago. His Majesty has refused to see them until you have arrived. I suggest you follow me." He turned on his heel and made his way up the stairs. Jane and Frank followed the candle lights like moths drawn to the flames. "Pets are not permitted onto the grounds," he remarked over his shoulder. "But I will allow it just this once, I suppose."

"I'm not a *pet*, bub," Frank said through gritted teeth. "Doing a heck of a job with the place, Jeeves. Really know how to welcome in a couple of-"

"Shhh!" Jane shot at him with furrowed brows. The last thing she wanted was to get on someone's nerves.

"I would have swept a bit had I known we were going to have company," Mr. Both said drolly.

"When was the last time you had guests?" Jane asked.

"Your friends were the first since His Majesty created me."

"How long ago was that?"

"About five-billion years ago. That's when I stopped counting, at least."

Jane and Frank looked at each other quizzically, but before they could ask any more questions, Mr. Both had opened a set of double doors at the top of the stairs. Inside was a large dining room decorated with statues and frescoes of dragons. On the table was a lit candelabra, which illuminated the room with an amber glow. Sitting around the table was Mrs. Macabre, Bram, and Arachne. They all let out a cry and ran towards Jane with a huge embrace.

"Thank Hades, you're alive!" Mrs. Macabre smiled and kissed her on the forehead.

"Thank Hades all of *you*, are alive!" Jane said, holding back tears.

"Who's that?" Arachne asked, raising an eyebrow and pointing at Frank.

"Name's Frank," the nightmare replied. "We just met," he cocked his head towards Jane.

"You're *amazing*!" Bram said in wonderment. He got down on his haunches to see Frank up closer. "Can I pet you?"

"Left ear is the sweet spot," Frank moved closer to him and allowed the boy to scratch behind his ear. He panted and licked him on the cheek in appreciation.

"As much as I enjoy a reunion," Mr. Both said, impatiently, "I must be attending to the kitchen. His Majesty will be waking shortly from his daily nap and will want to celebrate. Today is his birthday, after all." Mr. Both tore into Mr. Right and Mr. Left again and hopped through an exit at the corner of the room.

"Birthday?" Jane said to herself as she sat in one of the velvet chairs around the table. "That's quite the coincidence."

"We've been celebrating it for the past two days," Arachne sighed, getting into her chair as if it were another round of torture.

"Every day is his birthday," Mrs. Macabre said.

"Why is every day his birthday?"

"He can't remember when his real birthday is," Bram said, sitting next to her with Frank in his lap. "We asked Mr. Both the same question."

"Jane, my love," Mrs. Macabre said gently, "why did you run off like that?"

"I thought that after what happened with Catie and the bed bugs, that it would be safer for all of you if I didn't cause any more trouble," she said this with a sinking feeling in her chest. "But I. . . I didn't realize that I just got myself into *more* trouble."

"Darling," Mrs. Macabre said, holding her hand. "That was not your fault. We would have bound to get into danger in a place like this. Never think that you are a burden on us. You are a part of our spooky family. Without you, why, I don't know how it would ever be the same."

"Are you angry at me for running off?"

"Angry?" Mrs. Macabre gave a small smile. "No, of course not, love. Scared? Worried? Yes. But never mad. I could never be angry at you."

Tears welled in Jane's eyes. "I just hope the Fear King can help us."

"Help you with *what*?" A stern voice rang from the end of the hall as a pair of doors flew open. The Fear King's shadow loomed large over the entire room, like a giant made of darkness. As he walked closer to them, however, Jane saw that he was not a giant at all. He was a six year-old boy dressed in a velvet cut-away jacket with matching knee trousers. He also wore a fancy blouse with a large lace collar. A crown made out of paper sat crooked on his long dark hair. He did not walk into the room, but stomped, his heels clicking as they hit the marble floor. He reached his chair at the end of the table, which she only now noticed had two cushions, so that he was eye level with them all.

"Ya gotta be kiddin' me," Frank said.

"A dog," the Fear King looked at him with arms crossed. "A rather boring birthday present, but it will suffice."

"I'm not your dog," Frank growled at the boy. Before the Fear King could retort, the door in the corner banged open and in came Mr. Right and Mr. Left, wheeling in two carts. One was lined with empty glasses, the other sat a large cake adorned with acid green icing. A candle burned on the top of it.

"Apologies for the slight delay, Your Majesty," Mr. Right said in a panicked voice.

"He was off day dreaming again," Mr. Left mumbled, passing the glasses around the table.

"Oh, shut up, you!" Mr. Right shot back at him. "You're always blaming me for *your* mistakes!"

"Well, I wouldn't blame you if you were good at your job," Mr. Left hissed at his brother.

"CAKE!" The Fear King screamed, his eyes turning crimson for a moment.

"Yes, Your Majesty!" Mr. Both reconnected himself and lifted the birthday cake with both hands. He sat the thing down with a heave.

"SING!" The Fear King screamed again and they all began to sing. Mrs. Macabre, Arachne, and Bram droned on for the third time whereas Mr. Both put every ounce of energy into it. The Fear King took in a huge breath and blew out the candle with such a gust of air that it shook the entire dining room. They all had to hold on to the table at the sheer force of it. The candelabra went out, leaving them completely in the dark. Mr. Both pulled out a match and lit the extinguished candles again.

"Don't we get any plates, sir?" Jane asked, looking around the empty table. She shook the glass to make sure nothing was in it.

"It's my birthday," the Fear King said as he shoveled cake into his mouth with both hands. "And since it is my birthday, you get to watch me eat cake," he did not say this as if he was trying to be rude, but as if he did not know any better.

Bram rolled his eyes at her. "Uh. . . okay," Jane mustered. "Your Majesty, I have a request for you."

"They said you did," he pointed a sticky finger to the others. "I didn't want to know because I wanted it to be a surprise. A

BIRTHDAY SURPRISE!" He screamed with such glee that it frightened her. He giggled when he saw her jump.

"Yeah," Jane recovered herself. "You see, I came all the way from my world just to see *you*," she said, trying to play to his ego.

"Uh-huh," he said with his mouth full.

"I've been having horrible panic attacks where I come from and they've been awful to go through."

"Uh-huh," he did not look at her.

"Not to mention my sister, Catie, was stung by a bed bug. She's alive, but only by a medicine from Mrs. Macabre," she glanced at the witch who encouraged her to go on.

"That's sad," he said in a flat tone.

Jane's patience began to grow thin, but she did her best to keep cool. "Since then, I've nearly been eaten by vultures, cut open and examined, almost mauled to death, and would have drowned if it weren't for my furry friend, here. Now. Please, Your Highness. Will you help me cure my anxiety and save my sister?"

"No," the Fear King said, finishing the cake and wiping his mouth on the beautiful sleeve of his jacket.

11.
FACING THE
DRAGON

"N o?!" They all said in unison, aghast at the answer. Even Mr. Both seemed surprised, though he tried to hide it as best as he could.

"No," the Fear King repeated, licking his fingers, completely unfazed by their reactions.

"Why not? Jane asked with a lump forming in her throat. "You're the Fear King! You created this castle! The Nightmare Jungle! Why can't you do those other things?"

"I don't know how," he shrugged. "I can make scary things, but I don't know how to un-make them."

"So all of this walking, this danger, this-this whole journey was for *nothing*?" She nearly shrieked the last word, she was filling up with so much anger that she was nearly shaking.

"Not nothing!" The Fear King smiled with joy. "You can all stay here and be my friends!" They all stared at him in stunned silence. "My friends!" He said again as if they didn't hear him the first time. He let out a heavy sigh, leaning back in his chair. "You all can be my friends, so that I won't be alone."

"But, Your Majesty," Mr. Both piped up in a meek voice, "you have me."

"You're so booooring, though," the Fear King rolled his eyes at his butler, who lowered his head like a dog that was being scolded. "I want friends to play with and have birthday parties with and read stories together and-and. . . " His voice trailed off, trying to think of something else. "And that way you don't have to be afraid of anything ever again!" He pointed to Jane, as if this was an added bonus.

"What about my sister?" She asked flatly, unamused by his nonsense.

"I think the one, two, three, four, of you will be enough!" He said with a tone of reassurance.

"How long are we going to stay here?" Bram asked, a little frightened by how mad this whole situation had become.

"Forever and ever, of course!" The Fear King beamed with pride.

"What happens when they die?" Arachne asked, wanting to get this whole thing over with.

"What's that again?" The Fear King inquired.

"It's a mortal condition, Your Majesty," Mr. Body chimed in. "I believe it is when the physical body expires after a certain length of time."

"You mean they. . . break?" He was puzzled by this new found revelation.

"Precisely, Your Majesty."

The Fear King placed a finger to his chin and looked up for several moments, thinking to himself, until finally exclaimed with a snap of his fingers. "Then I'll get new friends! Just like when toys break and I have to make new ones."

"That's it!" Jane fumed, slamming her fists on the table. "We aren't going anywhere. We aren't going to be your friends.

In fact, I don't know why anyone would want to be your friend. You're not a king, you're a brat. An entitled, greedy, selfish brat! No one could *ever* be friends with such a horrible, horrible, *horrible* kid as you! Now, either you tell us how to fix me and my sister or you'll be stuck here ALONE FOREVER! GOT IT?" She was breathing like a steam engine, her face bright red. The others stared at her in shock, never having seen her so furious. Indeed, she was angry, but her anger combined with the fear of what would happen to her and Catie became a volatile mix.

The Fear King stared at her blankly for a moment, then began to sob. "THIS LITTLE GIRL IS BEING MEAN TO ME!" He wailed so loud that they all had to cover their ears. The castle shook with such a force that dust and bits of stone were falling from the ceiling. "MEAN! MEAN! MEAN! SHE DOESN'T WANNA PLAY WITH MEEEEEEEEEEEEE!"

"Would you SHUT! UP!" Jane screamed in his face through gritted teeth.

The Fear King immediately stopped screaming and his face changed to a naughty grin, as if he was keeping a secret. "Ohhhhhh, you've been a bad, bad, girl," He smiled wider, showing his teeth, which were now as sharp as knives. "If you won't be my friend, then *none* of you will." He began to tremble, making the table shake along with him. His skin began to grow black scales and his body was getting taller and larger by the second. His eyes turned red and a long forked tongue licked his teeth. His head grew longer and horns burst through his scalp, making his hair and crown disappear. An enormous tail grew behind him and long leathery bat wings erupted from his back. Until finally, a huge dragon stood at the center of the dinning hall.

"You are all on your own!" Mr. Both cried, trembling. He ran back to the kitchen door and promptly locked it from the inside.

The dragon blew out steam from its nostrils and gave them all a wicked grin. In the rubble of the dining table, Mrs. Macabre turned her cane into a broom and extended it. "Come on!" She cried and they all straddled the thing, they shot off like a rocket. The dragon roared and flew after them in return.

They burst out of the dining room doors and the interior of the castle was no longer the same. It was a collection of stairways and corridors going in every direction possible. Jane's head almost throbbed with confusion as she looked at the strange optical illusion. As the dragon followed them through the opening, breaking everything in its path, Mrs. Macabre chose a path at random and flew towards it.

The corridor that they had chosen went around and around in circles, the dragon chasing them over and over. They all felt dizzy until an opening appeared and they were soon in a chamber that was completely upside down. A large chandelier hung undisturbed from the ground, while chairs and tables stood on the ceiling. With every passing moment, the room was shattered into pieces by the dragon.

Next, a seemingly never ending gallery of portraits of the Fear King. Each one laughing maniacally as they flew past them. A door lead them through a room completely underwater, they all held their breath as quickly as they could. The dragon diving in and snorting bubbles behind them. Its body moving up and down, its tail swishing back and forth in the water.

They went through a wall of water, soaking wet into a hall of mirrors. Left right, up down, all they saw were their own reflections looking back at them as mirrors shattered behind them. There was no way out, so Mrs. Macabre made the executive decision to fly through a mirror and so they did.

Reflective glass shattered all around them as daylight greeted them on the other side. They let out a cry of joy, until the dragon's teeth gripped the end of the broomstick, sending them flying off of it. They hit the grass with a thud.

Jane looked up in horror as the dragon spat out the broom, it fell into the branches of a nearby tree. The dragon unfolded its enormous wings, like a black swan, and it broke through the castle, sending bricks and stones showering around it, leaving the castle in mere ruins.

"Uh, Mrs. Macabre?" Jane asked, backing away from the creature, as they all were. "Any ideas?"

"So sorry, my dear," Mrs. Macabre said through terrified breaths.

Jane's mind raced and all she could think of was pulling out the Fairy Godmother's compass. She did and the needle pointed directly at the dragon. *Of course it would*, she thought, annoyed.

The dragon stomped its thick claws into the grass, making the ground tremble. It made its way to them, Slowly but surely, inch by inch, toying with them to their doom. Its shape loomed so large, it nearly blocked out the light. Birds and beasts could be heard nearby fleeing in terror.

She didn't know why, but Jane finally blurted out, "You're scared!" The dragon stopped moving and looked at her, puzzled. "You-you heard me!" She tried her best to not sound scared herself. "You're just a scared little boy!"

The dragon moved back several paces, making a strange moaning sound in its throat. "Go on, Jane," Mrs. Macabre encouraged her after a glance. They all did.

"You're not as big and tough as you think you are!" Jane cried out, standing up. The dragon seemed to be growing smaller by the second. "I've seen scarier stuff in my school lunchroom!" She moved closer to it, the monster continuing to shrink. Were those tears coming out of those red eyes? "I can stand up to you any day of the week!" The dragon was now the size of her. "You know why? *Because I'm not afraid of you!*"

The dragon turned back into the Fear King, who was whimpering and sobbing. He cowered behind a fallen piece of stone. "P-P-please don't hurt me!"

Jane looked back at her friends who shared the same expression. "Hurt you?" She asked him. "Why would I-"

"Everyone is so-so *mean* to me!" The Fear King trembled. "They've hurt me so bad!"

Jane couldn't help but feel pity for the boy and got down next to him. She moved her hand towards him, but he flinched, as if she was going to strike him. "I'm not going to hurt you," she said softly. She gently placed her hand on his back as he was shaking like a leaf in the wind. "Will you tell me what's wrong?"

With a sniff and a quivering lip, he told his tale.

12.
THE FEAR
KING'S STORY

Once upon a time there was a little boy named Fear. He lived with his siblings Love, Life, and Death in No-Thing long ago. He felt at home in the blackness of No-Thing. Then their creator, Imagination, made Everything. He and his siblings were cast out all over as stars, moons, suns, and galaxies formed around them for infinity. Everything was so big that Fear began to feel lonely. He would often get bullied by a comet passing by or a black hole would shun him from conversation. When he was in No-thing, he felt safe and protected by his siblings. But now that they were so busy being part of the Everything, he was left to his own thoughts, which were plagued with anxieties and despair.

After traveling the Everything for millennia, he came across a strange realm called the Hallowland. It was so strange that it could not be found on any map. He quietly walked into it and was amazed by what he saw. A world with monsters, ghosts, and goblins! A place filled with all the things that bumped in the night. A place that offered a safe haven to all others that were shunned or misunderstood. Surely he could find a new family here!

But it was not to be. Ghosts would quiver at the mere sight of him, vampires locked themselves in their coffins when he strolled by, even a simple "Hello" from his lips would send a banshee screaming for their life. It had appeared that even monsters were afraid of Fear.

He found his brother Death on the river Styx and asked him to take him to the Afterlife. "I am afraid that is not possible, little brother," the Grim Reaper explained. "The Afterlife is reserved only for the Dead. We can never die for we are Eternal."

He wept. He buried himself deep underground where no one else could find him and cried himself to sleep every night. Who would ever dare play with Fear? Who would ever dare be Fear's friend? Who would ever dare accept Fear for who he was?

No one.

He was truly all alone in the universe. Then an idea came to him. If he couldn't find a home for himself, he would make one instead. So, he crawled his way out of the ground and planted a seed from the palm of his hand. It grew and grew until it became a jungle in the shape of a spiral. He then took some clay and sculpted every beast, bird, and creature the likes of which the Hallowland had never seen before. He would grow his own garden of Eden just for himself and then he would no longer be alone.

But instead of a garden, he had created a zoo. Fear was always the most wild and unpredictable of his siblings. He did not understand that if he created life, then it would live on its own. Instead of being his pets, the nightmares that he conjured soon went about their own business. Eating, sleeping, slithering, doing whatever they were born to do, except be friends with him.

He stomped his feet and cried out with anger, "*Fine!* If I can't have pets, I'll have a house!" So he took a single stone and multiplied it over and over until it formed an enormous castle. He filled it with as many rooms as he could think of, decorated it with as many works of art, furniture, and the like to make it the most grand and regal palace in creation. He lived there for several hundred years, playing with toys that he would make until they were broken or he grew bored of them. At which point, he would make new ones, play with them, brake them, then begin the cycle anew.

The boy was still lonely.

So he decided that he would create a servant. One that would do his bidding whenever he wanted, whatever he wanted. He took a bone, then grew a skeleton, which then grew organs, which then grew skin, which then grew a man. Then he thought, why have one butler when he could have two? He sliced the man down the middle, and thus one became two and two became one.

The butlers he named Mr. Both, Mr. Right, and Mr. Left were more than happy to serve Fear. They would read him bedtime stories, they would preform plays for him, each one playing a different character. He particularly loved a play called *King Lear*, though he thought the ending was wrong and decided to change it so that the King's daughter did not die and instead held a party for himself.

This gave Fear another idea. Though the butlers were doing wonderful at their jobs, he still felt a sense of loneliness that clawed at the deepest parts of his heart. He thought that the best way to get rid of this loneliness, was to make everyone love him. He had forgotten what Love was like since he had not seen his sibling for eons. He thought that love was about people serving him, and since he created the Nightmare Jungle and the castle, why shouldn't he be the Fear King?

He made himself a crown out of paper and ordered Mr. Both to make an announcement to the Hallowland that he was indeed the King of Fear and that everyone should love him for it. Instead they were all afraid of him. No one came to be his friend. No one came to play with him. No one even knocked on his front door.

Fear felt lonely again and decided that every day was his birthday. Since no one else would love him, he would treat every day as if it was His Day. Filled with cake, toys, and celebration in the castle that he built for himself with a servant that he made for himself.

But still the loneliness clawed at him. His castle slowly went to ruin, while the Fear King continued to be feared. No matter how much cake he had, no matter how many toys he played with, Fear was all alone.

Silence. They all stood around, looking at one another in shock and disbelief. Most of all Jane. As she watched the boy tremble and cry softly to himself, she thought of how wrong she was to have judged him. She had judged Fear's loneliness and despair as greedy, selfish, and cruel. But if she were to place herself into his skin, she could see how such feelings could come out that way.

After all, could you, dear reader, imagine what it would be like to live billions of years alone? Surely you could imagine one year or two, possibly three. But *billions*? One would wager that you've never counted to five hundred on your own, let alone a thousand, let alone a million, let alone a billion. You would have no concept of how such an existence would weigh on your heart and mind. So it would stand to reason that the weight of that pain would have to release itself somehow. That fear of never having a friend for all eternity. It was a never ending pain that Jane could relate to in a way.

When she began this adventure, she had believed that she was doing it for her own benefit. To help herself heal the pain that was deep inside of her, releasing itself in those awful panic attacks . But upon reflection, that wasn't entirely true. What she wanted was it to go away. A quick fix to make her feel better so that she wouldn't have to do the hard work of looking at her emotions straight in the face.

That was what the Nightmare Jungle taught her. Though the things that she had been through were terrible and terrifying, they did not compare to the horror of looking at herself. Healing is not done with a potion, a band aid, or a spell. It is a process that takes years, perhaps even a lifetime to fully take care of the wounds in our hearts.

Now apply that lifetime to billions of lifetimes and you will come close to how the Fear King felt. Of course he appeared unloveable because *he* thought he was unloveable.What else would you think if your siblings abandoned you and you were left to handle a universe that was so alien and strange to you?

It was a wonder he did not stay in the ground for all this time.

It came without warning. Jane immediately bent down and embraced him. She wrapped his arms around him as hard as she ever wrapped them around Catie or her parents wrapped around her when she was feeling at her worst. It was her birthday gift to him. The gift of connection.

"It's okay," she whispered in his ear. She felt him stiffen, as if confused by what was going on, but he then relaxed again.

"It's okay," she whispered again.

He stiffened. Then relaxed.

"It's okay."

He breathed in. He breathed out.

"It's okay."

He held tight. Then he let go.

Jane unwrapped herself from him. She looked at her friends and they had tears in their eyes. Frank tried to hide his, by looking away, but it was evident.

"Well, Your Majesty," Mrs. Macabre gave him a warm smile., summoning her broom with the snap of her fingers "It has been a pleasure meeting you. We would love to stay, but I am afraid we must be going. It is getting dark and I must find a remedy of some sort for Catherine."

"Thank you for celebrating my birthday with me," he smiled to them as they were leaving for the first time with true happiness.

"Oh, one more thing!" Jane said, quickly running back to him. She took out the compass from her pocket and handed it to him.

"What's this?" The Fear King asked, gazing at the device with wonder.

"It's something that you'll need," she said taking her hand and laying it on top of his.

"What do I do with it?"

"I don't have the answers for you. That's something you'll have to figure out on your own."

"But. . . being on my own is scary."

"It's only scary if you're afraid of yourself."

He smiled at her with both confusion and joy at the same time.

Just before she crossed back into the trees, Jane turned around and saw Mr. Both rising from the rubble and shaking the dust off of his suit. He and the Fear King looked at the compass, trying to figure out how it worked, as she had done when the Fairy Godmother had given it to her. A swelling in her chest reminded her of one of her panic attacks, but this swelling was not the swelling of fear that she had grown so used to. It was the swelling of compassion. Compassion for not just the Fear King, but for herself.

"Where did you get that compass from?" Bram asked.

"My fairy godmother gave it to me," Jane smiled as her friend looked at her, confused.

They returned to Frank's cave and set up camp there. As they all went through the tent, Jane saw Mrs. Mirth struggling to close the front door of the manor.

"I'm terribly sorry," she grunted, trying to close the door with her shoulder as claws and hands flung various products her way, "but we're not interested in buying *anything*!" She slammed the door shut as a flyer for a Two-Headed Skin Care Routine floated onto the floor. She let out an enormous sigh and noticed them all coming in. "Jane!" She cried out and flung her arms around her. "We were worried sick about you!"

"I'm so sorry!" Jane said, accepting the hug with gratitude.

"As long as you're here, that's all that matters, dear," she smiled as Mrs. Macabre gave her a peck on the cheek. "Oh!" Her face lit up. "Do I have a surprise for you!" She quickly grabbed Jane and Bram's arms and ran into the kitchen.

There, sitting at the table, was Catie. She was nursing a cup of tea, but other than looking extremely tired, she was all right. Jane and Bram burst into tears of joy and ran to her, hugging her and kissing her head.

"Easy! Easy!" Catie laughed, as she was nearly knocked off her chair. "I'm still not one-hundred percent yet."

"I don't. . . " Mrs. Macabre said, mouth agape. "How. . . When. . ." It was not very often that Mrs. Macabre was at a loss for words, so you know how stunned she truly was.

"There aren't any Hallowland remedies for bed bug venom," Mrs. Mirth beamed. "But there are a few Northern potions that Grandmama Mirth taught me years ago. I had completely forgotten them and suddenly it hit me while you were gone. I just gave her a cold cloth on the head and a few tears of a dove on her wound and she woke up an hour or so later!"

Jane was gobsmacked This entire time, all that trouble, all that time spent worrying, was solved by something she would never have considered. She realized that her fear was just that, fear. It was a feeling, an emotion, not an actual thing. Though it felt real, it was entirely of her own making. The irony of it all was almost unbearable. If her backpack hadn't ripped at the exact moment, she would have been food for Ms. Rabies' children. If the lightning bolt hadn't struck that tree, the Good Doctor would have ripped her apart. If Frank hadn't happened to be there at the right time, the Abyss would have swallowed her whole It seemed that hope can come in the most unlikely of ways.

Another thought hit her, *of course* things would not have been better without her. *Of course* all of those frightening experiences with Catie were not her fault, they were just frightening experiences, as common in life as a rain storm. *Of course* Catie and her should stick together. They are the Gracey twins, after all. And like all twins, they are two halves of the same brain. One cannot live without the other.

Jack Lantern came running into the kitchen. "Oh, my goodness, I am so, so happy to see-WHAT IS THAT THING?" He screamed, pointing a shivering finger at Frank.

"The name's Frank," the nightmare replied without offense. "I'm a friend of Jane, over there. Or is the other one Jane? I don't know. One of 'em. Nice place ya got here? Mind if I stay?"

They all looked at Mrs. Macabre. "Well, I'm more of a cat person, myself," she said as Frank lifted an eyebrow. "But I'm sure we can accommodate dogs, as well."

They all laughed, save for Jack, who chuckled nervously.

The children returned to their homes later that night. Mrs. Mirth had given Catie a vial of dove tears so that she could place it on her wound. She said that she should be fully healed in three days or so. Along the way back, Jane and Bram told the other Gracey sister about all that happened, her head nearly spinning trying to keep up.

Once the Gracey twins had returned to their real bedroom, a strange sensation occurred to Jane. A part of her expected to feel unsafe in the room, as if a monster was going to burst out of the closet or the floor might cave in on them, but there wasn't. There was no feeling of anticipation or dread, there was no bracing for impact, there was only stillness. A stillness inside of herself that could only be achieved if she wasn't worrying about the future or feeling sad about the past. It reminded her of when she meditated in Frank's cave. It was the stillness of This Moment, Right Now.

"Still not happy that you left to find the Fear King on your own," Catie told her as they got back into their pajamas.

"I know," she replied, the guilt still stinging deep within her. It would be a wound that would take more than anything Mrs. Macabre or Mrs. Mirth ever had to heal.

"I hope you found what you were looking for," Catie grumbled, getting into bed.

"You know, I think I did," Jane smiled and, even with her back towards her. She sensed that Catie was smiling too.

13.
COMPASS OF
YOUR HEART

When the Gracey twins woke up the next morning, Jane knew what had to be done. She waited to do it after school, a day that was absent of any panic attacks. Once she, Catie, and her parents were at the dinner table, she told them what had been warring in her mind for the past several months. The panic attacks, the negative thoughts, everything. Mr. and Mrs. Gracey were both shocked to hear this news, of course. Not only because they wished with all their hearts that neither of their daughters would go through so much suffering, but also because they had no idea that it was going on.

"I can't believe I didn't *see* it," Mrs. Gracey said, wiping tears from her eyes. Perhaps that's the greatest fear a parent suffers. Not that harm would come to their child, but that they did not see it. That something wrong was right in front of their faces and for whatever reason, they could not see that their child was in pain.

Catie held Jane's hand the entire time.

A week later, Jane stepped into the office of a therapist. She was quite surprised by how relaxing the experience was. Her therapist, Dr. Solis, was not even thirty years old and greeted her as if she was meeting a new friend, not a patient. Jane did not feel poked or prodded by Dr. Solis' questions as if she were some science experiment but concerned for and cared about. Even though their session only lasted an hour, she felt held by this person in ways that she hoped she could do for herself one day.

Now, it should be noted that Jane did not disclose her problems through literal fact. She could never bring up Mrs. Macabre or the Hallowland to Dr. Solis lest she be put on a hundred different medications. Instead, she disguised these facts as emotions. Instead of recounting the helplessness and despair that she felt in the grip of the Weeping Widow, she talked about how she felt sad and out of control of her own life most of the time. Instead of mentioning the tyrannical rule of Father Christmas of the North, she told Dr. Solis of how she felt like she was being judged at school. And of the Fear King and the Nightmare Jungle? I'm sure you have guessed that that belonged under the subject of anxiety.

They were not lies, exactly. If you are seeing a therapist and trust them, then you should be as honest with them as you feel comfortable with. Instead what came out of her was Truth. Something that was deeper than Fact. The truth was how she felt about those adventures in the Hallowland, not what literally took place there. After all, your idea of what actually happened in any given situation may be different from someone else's because you and them feel different things. Emotions are true, whereas facts are just reality.

J ane stood on the front porch of Mrs. Macabre's manor. She was looking up at the moon as it cast a purple glow with thousands of stars twinkling around it. She wondered if Love or Life was watching from one of the stars, smiling down on their brother Fear for finally going down a path of his own. The sounds of Mrs. Macabre cooking dinner and her other friends laughing inside warmed her heart. She had missed the sounds of her spooky family so much in the depths of the jungle.

She gasped as her eyes caught something. Not far beside the lake that the house sat beside, she saw two twinkling eyes next to a tree. She thought for a moment that they were a couple of stars from above, but she then realized that it was the Fairy Godmother again. Jane quickly looked behind her to see if anyone was coming, but she only saw the faint glow of candlelight from the cracked door. She ran down the steps and towards the tree,

"Hey!" She softly called to the Fairy Godmother as she caught up with her. "What are you doing here?" The Fairy Godmother merely stood still and smiled warmly at her. "Who are you? Really, I mean?" Jane quickly asked, the one out of a thousand questions that spun through her mind leapt out of her mouth.

"Fairy Godmother," she said in a tone that sounded almost like a question. As if she herself did not understand what Jane was asking.

"Why don't the others remember you?" Jane pointed to the manor behind her. "When you gave me the compass?"

"Fairy Godmother is seen when Fairy Godmother wants to be seen," she shrugged slightly.

Jane felt a creeping sense of frustration as she remembered the compass. "Why did you give me that thing, anyways? All it did was get me into scary situations and-and. . . well, you'd think finding the castle would be a lot easier than all *that!*" She said hotly.

"Change is frightening," the Fairy Godmother replied like she was describing the weather, which in turn made Jane more angry.

She opened her mouth to fire some sassy remark at the strange woman, but she couldn't. She was too busy thinking about what she had just heard. Yes, it was true that all she had been through was frightening, but it was also true that she had changed. She had changed for the better, in fact. Or, rather, the Fact of the matter was that her time in the Nightmare Jungle was scary and she would not want to experience it again. But the Truth of the matter was that if she had not had gone through those scary things, she would have never made the choices that lead to this exact moment or deciding to see a therapist or even listen to the Fear King's story. She realized that she could go through something terrible and yet the responsibility was on her to either be gentle with herself or not. She could think about the hundred other ways she could have avoided them, but the Fact was that those awful things happened to her. To argue with reality was pointless. It was what she took away from those experiences that mattered. Her brain fizzed like an open can of soda as she tried to wrap her head around such a concept.

"Compass is here," the Fairy Godmother placed a hand to her own chest, sensing her puzzlement. "That is change."

It clicked. That was what she had *really* discovered in the Nightmare Jungle. Before, she had wanted to find the compass outside of herself. What she needed was to find the compass within her own self. No one could "fix" her problems but her. "Thank you," Jane breathed out with gratitude. "Will I see you again?"

"Time is a wheel," the Fairy Godmother said, making a large circle with her arm in the air in front of her. Before Jane could ask her what she meant, a voice interrupted them.

"Jane?" Jack Lantern said from behind her. "Who are you talking to?" He asked.

"I was just-" she turned to him and then back to the Fairy Godmother, but she was gone. Typical. "I was just talking to myself," she smiled back at him.

"Oh," Jack said with a sigh of relief, a puff of smoke coming out of the cut of his mouth. "I thought you were talking to the Weeping Widow again or something! Mrs. Macabre wanted me to tell you that dinner is ready."

They both walked back to the manor. "Jack?" Jane asked, noticing the uncomfortable silence. "Is there something you want to talk about?"

"I just… I was wondering… " Jack struggled with his words as the straw rustled in his wringing gloved hands. "I want to know how you did it?"

"Did what?" She stopped at the foot of the stairs, looking up at him.

"You know. . . talk to the Fear King! I mean he's so-" Jack looked around as if to see if someone was watching them. "Scary," he whispered.

"I just talked to him."

"Yes, yes!" He cried impatiently. "But how were you so *brave*?"

Jane thought for a moment. "I don't think it had anything to do with being brave. I didn't fight him or stand up to him, I just listened to him. When I was afraid, I never listened to myself or anyone else. But now that I am, I think I can understand things better."

"So, that's it? Just listen to people and you won't be afraid?"

"No. I think I'm still going to be afraid."

"Then what was the point of all that?" He pleaded.

"I'm not afraid of being afraid anymore," the words came out of Jane's mouth so easily it surprised her.

Jack stood still for a moment. "Remember when you and Catie once told me about how being afraid was what made me special?"

"Yes," Jane laughed a little, remembering.

"Well, do you think that if I can learn to stop being afraid of being afraid then maybe I won't be so afraid of myself anymore?"

"Maybe."

"But that's so. . . so. . . *hard* and *scary*!" He shivered.

" I think it's worth trying," Jane smiled at him and Jack's candle glowed brightly inside his head. They both walked inside the manor with the stars bidding them goodnight from above.

The Mrs. Macabre Chronicles will continue.

Don't miss out!

Visit the website below and you can sign up to receive emails whenever Austin Ray Bouse publishes a new book. There's no charge and no obligation.

https://books2read.com/r/B-A-XPIK-EDXOC

BOOKS 2 READ

Connecting independent readers to independent writers.

About the Author

Austin(They/Them) is a writer and practicing witch living in central Texas. They are the author of *The Mrs. Macabre Chronicles*. They are non-binary and have a form of cerebral palsy. They plan on keeping it that way.

Read more at https://linktr.ee/austiniswriting.

9 798223 506942